BOOKMARKED FOR CRIME

A SHELF INDULGENCE COZY MYSTERY

S.E. BABIN

Previously published by Sweet Promise Press - 2019

Published by Oliver-Heber Books

0 9 8 7 6 5 4 3 2 1

WANT TO KEEP UP WITH SHERYL?

You can grab a FREE set of stories here if you sign up for my newsletter.

Or, you can click the kitty cat and follow Sheryl online at sebabin.com. She emails only when she has a new release or has messed something up. And even then she sometimes forgets...

ONE

I gasped. "You're cheating!" I didn't know how. I didn't know why. But I knew for certain Daniel Jensen was cheating at chess.

A small smile curled over his generous lips as he moved his Bishop into place right beside one of my last pawns. "There's no cheating without proof," he said sagely.

My mouth fell open. The cheek! "If I know you're cheating and you know you're cheating, how could there be no cheating?"

His lips curled into a full-on grin. "Because you don't know *how* I'm cheating and if you can't figure it out, then I maintain there is no cheating to be found."

I'd hung out with Daniel several times over the last few weeks and found him to be witty, engaging, intelligent, and a dirty, lying cheater when it came to chess. And he was right. I couldn't figure out how he was doing it.

We sat in his library, a place I never wanted to be without. This place gave the Beast's library a run for its money. Floor to ceiling bookshelves lined every wall, crammed with books both modern and classic. The floor was a burnished mahogany wood, scarred with furniture moving and the ravages of time. His house was massive, a mansion in every meaning of the word, but I'd come to learn that Daniel occupied very little of it. He spent most of his time in this room, the kitchen, and the small living area toward the front of the house. The rest remained mostly untouched but kept tidy by a biweekly housekeeper who ducked in and out and took her payment through a cash app.

Daniel was a famous author, though he had none of the trappings of fame that I could see. He was introverted but clever and had figured out how to minimize contact with just about everyone. We'd met when he came in to buy a rare book from me, and I thought it was a one off until the same book became an important piece of evidence in a crime. I'd tracked him down, we hit it off, and now I put up with Daniel cheating at chess on a semi-regular basis. We'd started with book dates and dinner. I picked up food and he provided wine. We ate, drank, and then remained mostly silent while we read through our selection. When we finished, we chatted and sometimes argued about it. Then we'd moved to sometimes playing chess and me always losing. But now that I knew he was cheating, I at least knew why he kept winning. I'd figure it out, so help me.

"Have you thought any more about moving?" I asked.

Him giving up this library would pain me forever, especially since it was my suggestion he scale down.

Daniel shrugged. "The security here is good. I like the library and I know you do too. A regular house would never provide the kind of room for all of this." He swept his hand in the air, encompassing the hundreds, potentially thousands of books in his collection. A sigh escaped me.

"It would be a shame to lose it."

His dark eyes glittered in the low light. "But I do have an idea."

My eyes narrowed. "Should I be afraid?"

He chuckled. "Not at all. I have all this land around here, and I'm not doing anything with it."

I tilted my head. "And?"

"And maybe I should build what I want on it and open the house as something of a museum."

I gaped at him. "You'd let people traipse through your private property and put their hands all over these books?"

Daniel laughed. "I'd let them traipse through for a charitable donation and hire someone to keep it running smoothly and who would keep the books safe."

"But what about the library?"

Daniel moved his queen into position. "Checkmate."

I growled. "You dirty, cheating dog."

He laughed under his breath. "I'd build another house. One suited to my taste."

I was still frowning down at the king I'd tipped over as my brain struggled to figure out how he'd beaten me once again. "I'm not sure we can still be friends if you're a cheater and libraryless."

"First of all, *libraryless* is not a word. Second, I'd build a new one."

My gaze flicked up. He leaned forward, a dark lock of hair falling over one eye. I'd tried not to notice how handsome Daniel was. He was the complete package. Tall, dark, handsome, and just enough of a geek for me to have developed a crush over the time I'd known him. But Daniel rarely dated anyone because of his celebrity status. I hadn't known who he was when I met him, but it's because I was somewhat of a Luddite with popular culture. I wouldn't risk ruining our burgeoning friendship over something so silly as a crush, so I tamped down those feelings and had somewhat convinced myself that Daniel was unobtainable. In some ways, he was, and that had to be enough. I would never want him to think I was getting close to him because of money. I certainly wouldn't own a bookshop in a small town if money was all that important to me. I did well enough to pay my bills and sometimes if I sold a rare book, more than enough to pay my bills, but I'd never be rich like Daniel Jensen unless I won the lottery.

This was not including the hefty deposit still sitting in my bank account left to me by Heather, the woman Daniel and I had helped a while back. To thank me, she'd deposited a large sum of money in my bank account, unbeknownst to me, then promptly took her family and disappeared off the map. With a net worth of over 250 million, I would have probably done the same.

Every time I opened my bank account, my mouth went dry. I didn't have a quarter of a billion dollars, but my bank account no longer held merely chump change. I could pay off the loan on the store and my mortgage if I wanted to and still have enough money to invest and live comfortably off of for a few years. I'd never once had this amount of money, so to see it every time I logged in made me a little breathless. For once, I didn't have to worry about a lean month at the store.

After the police closed Heather's case and the mineral rights landed back with her, I took a month off from the shop, with Harper's permission, of course. But before I did, I'd given her another healthy raise. Harper was now probably the most well-paid bookstore attendant in the country. She deserved every penny, too. Who else would put up with their boss chasing murderers and criminals across town lines? No one except for Harper.

"Earth to Dakota." Daniel peered at me over his wire-rimmed glasses.

I jerked my attention back. "Sorry," I muttered.

"Lost in thought again?"

I sighed. "I'm heading back to work on Monday."

He smiled, not fooled for a second. "And still worrying about the money in your account?"

Daniel was the only one I'd told. Not even Harper knew about the deposit Heather had given me. I didn't know why I'd told him, but I guess I figured he had enough money not to treat me any differently. And he hadn't.

"You know," he said, pushing his glasses up the bridge

of his nose, "she gave the money for services rendered. You almost single-handedly solved that case and made Heather a very rich woman in the process. I think I'd be more surprised if she *hadn't* given you something in return. Don't feel guilty, Dakota. Use it. It won't do anything sitting in your account. Invest it, pay some bills." He shrugged and sat back, his eyes sparkling at the overturned king. "Maybe take some chess lessons."

A surprised laugh bubbled from me. "Funny." I poured us both another small glass of wine and sat back against the surprisingly comfortable couch. "I didn't grow up poor," I confessed, "but there were some lean months where we had to penny pinch. Everything is fine now, but I remember those times and how it felt to watch my mother stress over something she couldn't really control."

He nodded. "I can't say I completely understand, but I did do my best to make it without my father's money." Daniel shrugged. "Of course, I'm back here now because of an inheritance, but I can honestly say I never wanted it. I worked like a dog to get the book contracts I have and the first few were basically peanuts to what they are now, but it took years of hard work to get me there." Daniel leaned over and put his hand on top of mine. His palm was warm and calloused. Not the typical hands of a writer, but I knew for a fact he had a private garden in the back of the house he maintained himself. I'd been the recipient of a few baskets of fruit and vegetables he'd grown. "Take the money in the spirit she gave it. As services rendered. You put yourself in danger for them. Few people would have done that."

I nodded and swallowed hard, overcome with his blessing and the hand that still rested over my own. Daniel Jensen was a difficult man to dislike and an even more difficult man not to become attracted to. I had a few men swirling around me, though Hardy was no longer in that mix. I'd rejected him after his brusque dismissal during the last case. We hadn't spoken since, and it occasionally felt like I was missing a limb. We'd grown close since I'd opened the store, but I didn't think he'd ever accept me as I was, and I realized how important to me it was, so I canceled our date right before I'd taken vacation. Harper had called me a week into it and told me Hardy had stopped by, but he didn't leave a reason for his visit and hadn't been back since.

I did not call him or reach out. The way my life was going now, I figured I'd see him soon enough anyway.

"Thank you. I could pay off the store if I wanted to."

Daniel's eyes widened. "Are you thinking about it?"

I nodded. "Tattered Pages would be mine, free and clear."

"Few people can claim they own 100% of their business. Banks do a brisk business with commercial loans around here."

"Maybe I could build a small apartment upstairs for those evenings when I stay too long," I mused.

Daniel grimaced at that. "No one should work that

hard, but at minimum, maybe make a small place for Poppy to stay."

Speaking of the cantankerous cat, Poppy lay curled on top of a small, discarded pile of paperbacks, right in front of a window. Filtered light streamed through, highlighting the white of her belly as she laid on her back, sound asleep. I smiled at her and shook my head. She liked Daniel. Way more than I thought she would, and she seemed to understand when I said I was coming over. Poppy would yowl and screech until I picked her up and plopped her into her car hammock. Then she'd jump out of the car when we arrived and sit quietly at his doorstep and wait for me to ring the bell. When Daniel answered, she'd rush through his legs and make herself comfortable in the library.

He stopped saying anything about it after the first visit and now kept a selection of cat treats in the kitchen for her.

Like I said. Daniel was the complete package so far.

"An apartment would be nice for festival weeks, though," I mused.

Daniel chuckled. "Silverwood and their festivals."

He wasn't wrong. The town loved their festivals. We had one for every holiday and then some. The annual Valentine's Day festival was close, but Silverwood wouldn't call it by the holiday. According to Trudy, it wasn't clever enough, and the tourists counted on the kitschiness of Silverwood to make their Instagram profiles pop. Whatever that meant. This year it was the annual Lovebird Fest, and the number of cardboard hearts going up all over the city was borderline nauseating.

I usually looked forward to all the town events, but this year, like the many years before, I'd be single. Valentine's Day wasn't the best holiday to be single during, but it was par for the course for me. I'd scratched Cole from my list two cases ago, and we'd finally settled into a new and tentative friendship again.

There was still Everett, but I rarely saw him, and I suspected he was more intrigued by my sleuth skills than me as a person. He'd dubbed me the "book slinging sleuth," which amused him to no end, but we'd still settled into a somewhat easy friendship and professional relationship as he was the acquiring editor at a mystery imprint, and I was always eager to peruse his new titles. We'd had dinner together a while ago, but it was while he was trying to sell me something, so maybe he shouldn't be on my list. Perhaps he used his good looks to entice small town bookstore owners into buying too many of his new titles.

Regardless, it seemed like singlehood was here to stay, and I'd better get used to it. "Are you coming to the Lovebird Fest?"

Daniel grimaced, and I couldn't help but laugh. "You're asking a hermit writer if he wants to subject himself to hordes of people and various versions of red desserts?"

I sighed. "Sounds wonderful, doesn't it?"

He snorted and started tucking the chess pieces back into their custom box. "Hardly."

"Not even Trudy's cherry pie can convince you?"

He smiled, a flash of strong white teeth. "Too peopley, Dakota." His gaze met mine. "Unless you're asking me."

I blinked. "Erm."

"*Are* you asking me?"

"Like a date?" I squeaked.

Daniel's eyebrows went up. "Is that what two single, attractive people do sometimes?" His voice was mock innocent.

My cheeks colored with embarrassment. "Um. I don't want to put you out. I, um, just thought maybe..." I grabbed my purse and stood, setting the wineglass down on the small coffee table that held the chess board. "I shouldn't have said anything." I spun to Poppy and scooped her up in my arms. "Thanks for the chess game," I blurted right before I rushed out of his house.

"Dakota!" Daniel called as he rushed after me, his voice exasperated.

"Bye!" I called and jogged down the steps and to my car.

He didn't chase me down the steps, but instead leaned against one of the stone pillars on his massive porch. A frown rested on his face as he watched me drive away.

"Idiot," I muttered. "Why am I such a dummy?"

Poppy, who lay on the seat beside me, yowled in protest as if to ask me the same question.

TWO

The embarrassment stayed with me all weekend. Daniel tried to call a couple of times, but I let it go to voicemail. Every time I thought about it, I wanted to curl up in the fetal position and die. I couldn't avoid him forever, but I could *definitely* avoid him for a while.

I pulled into the shop and sat in my vehicle for a moment, watching the still quiet downtown. It was early, but I had a lot to do today before the shop opened. Trudy's shop was open, so I slid out of the car and headed over there.

Walking into Sprinkle Heaven felt like walking straight into one of Trudy's cinnamon scented hugs. Stress fell away as soon as the scent of coffee and chocolate hit me. It was too early for cake, though Trudy would be appalled if I said that out loud, but it was never too early for a latte and a muffin.

"Dakota!" Trudy gasped. She untied her apron and

rushed over to me, gathering me into a hug. "It feels like it's been years!"

It hadn't, but I'd made myself scarce over the last few weeks. When I wasn't hanging out with Daniel, I was in the house perfecting pasta recipes and bingeing all the shows I'd been working too much to finish watching. It was heaven, but that was the thing about vacations, wasn't it? They always ended.

She held me at arm's length and studied me for a moment. "Hmm. No dark circles. No stress frown. Your vacation must have been good!"

I thanked the heavens that Daniel lived in Candlelight Springs because if he were here, the entire town would have us married off and honeymooning by now. "It was great. I spent a lot of time cooking and a lot of time in front of the television."

Trudy harrumphed and ushered me over to the counter. "Sounds amazing. The other two stores are open now and I'm pulled in a hundred different directions every single day." Her red hair was tied up in a messy bun on top of her head and she wore a pair of leggings with a long tunic shirt over them. Sturdy shoes and bright jewelry completed her look, but it didn't match with the lines bracketing her mouth and at the edges of her eyes.

"You okay?" I asked as she made me a latte. I didn't have to tell her what I wanted anymore. I came in here so much I'm surprised the other customers didn't call out my name as I walked to the register.

She gave me a faint smile. "Just tired. Nothing to worry

about. I've been looking for someone to help out in the other two shops, but finding reliable help isn't as easy as it used to be." Sympathy panged within me. I'd struck gold when Harper wandered into my shop. As far as I was concerned, she was irreplaceable and if she ever left me, I wondered if my store would collapse around my ears.

"Want me to put a notice up in the shop?" I had a bulletin board where I posted miscellaneous notices and event flyers.

She handed over the drink. "That would be amazing. I'll send you a text with what I'm looking for. I'm paying better than average, but the workload will be high for the first few months while we work out all the kinks. Then it should settle into something normal and not so crazy. It would be a good job for someone just getting out of college and in between jobs, though I'd love to have someone who would commit to a minimum of six months." She frowned. "Actually, I think I could offer a bonus after the six-month mark. Preferably, I'd love to have a long-term employee."

"I'll see what I can do."

"Thanks, honey." Trudy motioned for me to follow her back to the kitchen. I hesitated, only because my vacation resulted in my jeans being just a touch difficult to button this morning. Saying no to Trudy's desserts was physically impossible for me, though.

"I made this as a special February treat. It will only be in this shop, though." She led me behind the commercial mixer to the tray holding a dozen different desserts. Trudy chose a tray in the middle.

"I figured cinnamon would be the best bet for the month. You know, those red hot cinnamon candies."

I wrinkled my nose. "I like real cinnamon better. Those candies remind me of the craft store brooms that go up every Christmas."

Trudy laughed. "And it's all you can smell until your nose finally clears up hours later!" She tugged on plastic gloves and cut a piece from the large, rectangular tray. I didn't know what it was, but it was layered like a pastry.

"What is it?" I asked as I accepted the plate and fork she offered me.

Trudy peered at her offering. "I don't quite know. I came back here after being on my feet all day. Dead tired and three glasses of wine later, this is what I came up with."

I poked at it with my fork. It looked like a cheese Danish but not quite. There was a layer of something that looked like pastry cream, but with a light brown tinge to it. The pastry was almost like croissant dough, tender and flaky, and Trudy had lightly striped a white icing all over it and sprinkled cinnamon and sugar on top. I sniffed and sighed. It smelled like Christmas in a coffee shop.

"Don't keep me waiting," Trudy said. "I haven't been brave enough to try it yet."

"Trudy!"

She snickered. "Don't worry. I wrote everything down, which surprised me after all that wine. Who knew I could make such awesome pastry cream under the influence?"

I couldn't help but laugh. Cutting into the flaky dough,

I made sure to get some of the pastry cream on my fork and took a bite.

Coffee, cinnamon, and a hint of vanilla icing exploded in my mouth. "I don't know why I was nervous about that one," I admitted as I swallowed. "This is amazing, Trudy. Perfect for breakfast. The pastry is amazing, and the cream is just enough and not overwhelming." I took a sip of my latte. "I think you have a hit on your hands."

Trudy deflated in relief. "I was worried about this one. I had the radio roaring, the wine open, and I was dead on my feet."

"Apparently, being tired enough to hallucinate worked in your favor." I took another bite and tried not to moan in delight. Coffee pastry cream. Who would have thought? I didn't even know it existed, but now that I did, Trudy was going to have to fork over the goods for a while. "Oh! Before I forget." I set my plate down and dug into my purse. Pulling out a hardback, I handed it over to her. "This is the newest offering. Everett said it's amazing. He expects it to shoot up the charts."

Her eyes sparkled as she took the book from me. "Everett, huh?" She grinned and looked down at the title. "I just finished the last one you gave me. So good," she sighed. "The murderer creeped me out so much I kept a nightlight on in my bedroom for a week afterward!" Trudy grinned. "But...going back to Everett..."

I rolled my eyes at her. "You know what he does." I studied my nails. "He's only interested in me for my bookstore."

Trudy snorted at that. "Sure he is, Dakota. Just like a few other bachelors I know."

"Everett and I are only friends." My life scared him a little, I think. To be honest, it scared me too, sometimes.

"What about Hardy?"

My shoulders stiffened. "Hardy and I are only friends, too." Whether that was still true remained to be seen.

She gave me a long look. "I haven't seen him around lately." Her tone was light, but her meaning was clear.

"I've been on vacation, but I'm sure he's busy too."

"Mmm," Trudy said.

I took another sip of my latte and polished off the pastry before tossing a ten on the counter. "I gotta run. It's my first day back at the shop and there's a lot to do."

Trudy pushed the ten back at me. "Your money is no good here."

Sighing, I tucked it back into my purse. "Fine. Enjoy the book," I called out as I headed out of the kitchen. "No spoilers! I haven't read it yet."

"The bad guy never wins!" Trudy called back.

I chuckled, even though I knew sometimes they did.

TATTERED PAGES SAT in the middle of downtown, sandwiched between Trudy's shop and *Olive Twist!*, Jen's flavored olive oil store. Trudy's started out as a place to get the best cupcakes in town, but her genius could not stay dimmed. Soon she branched out into all kinds of delicious things. One which was still making me warm and fuzzy as

I puttered around the store getting things ready to open. I'd let Harper have the day off. I wanted to get back into the swing of things and have a relatively quiet day, and Harper needed to run some errands. She'd picked up a forty-hour workweek after her most recent raise, but she'd also just bought a house and ended up with some unexpected expenses.

I usually did more than forty hours, though for a while I'd been busy chasing down criminals, which cut way into my work time. All the more reason to have someone like Harper around. I wandered over to the coffee and tea stand and saw a note scrawled in her neat hand.

Earl Gray Creme from a new tea shop that just opened! It's divine.

I preferred coffee over tea but still enjoyed a cup now and then. Curious, I opened the small bag she'd left and inhaled. Hints of vanilla, lavender, and bergamot drifted up.

"Oh," I gasped in delight. I'd just bought a temperature-controlled kettle a few weeks ago and had barely used it before I'd taken off, so I set it up at 195 degrees for black tea and let it do its thing. It would stay at that temperature until I turned it off, so I tucked a bag into my favorite mug and went off to do something else while the water heated.

I FLIPPED the sign to *Open* and dispensed water into the mug before heading back over behind the register to wait. It was Monday so it could be a slow day, but sometimes I was surprised at the tourist traffic pouring through, even during the early part of the week. I'd set up a stand with the newest hardcover I'd given Trudy. The book was called *Her Darling Dead* by a debut author I'd never heard of. The blurb talked about a wife stalking her husband after she found out he was having an affair, only for him to wind up dead and her the prime suspect. Everett said the author was a little like Gillian Flynn, so I wasn't sure if I'd read it or not. She had the best characters, but goodness they were flawed.

I'd wait for Trudy to tell me how it was before I picked it up.

The bell over the door jingled a few minutes later, announcing the presence of an older woman with a short teenage girl who did not look pleased to be entering my store.

"Hi!" I called as the door clicked shut behind them. "Welcome to Tattered Pages. I'm Dakota. If you're looking for anything in particular, please let me know. Otherwise, I'll just leave you to browse."

The woman gave me a thin smile, and the teenager ignored me. Shrugging, I went back to my notepad and sketched out everything I needed to do for the week. With the festival coming up, I had to do a window display. There were a lot of upcoming romances, and the current trend was adorable, bright illustrated covers. I could find some good ones with pink and red covers and build the display around those. Frowning, I pulled up the current list of bestsellers only to come up with a few I wasn't sure would work.

"You promised!"

I jerked out of my research at the harsh tone coming from the back.

"I did no such thing," the older woman hissed. "You are embarrassing me. Lower your voice or we'll head back to the hotel for the rest of the day."

"But I love him!" the girl wailed.

I chewed on my lip. Fortunately, there were no other customers in, but this was definitely not an argument I should overhear. Just as I was about to get up and head back to the office, the bell jingled again, and the voices cut off abruptly.

Hardy Cavanaugh walked in, and his presence sucked all the air out of the room. When I first met him, he had more of a sense of humor about things. As time passed, his countenance grew grimmer. Or maybe it was me bringing him down. Who knew?

The woman and teen came back up to the register and plopped a couple of books down. My gaze skimmed over Hardy, but he went straight over to the new display and picked up the hardcover.

"Will that be all?" I asked when my tongue came unglued from the roof of my mouth.

"That's all," she said. The woman's eyes were rimmed with red, as if she'd been crying. She was pretty but faded, as if she'd been a rose exposed to the harsh sun for too long. She had dark hair graying at the temples and faded blue eyes. Her hands shook slightly as she took out her card to pay. My gaze slid to the girl wearing a mulish expression. She had to be related. Either a daughter or a niece. Her hair was ebony black, and she had the woman's blue eyes, though hers was much brighter.

Two books rested on the counter.

What to Expect When You're Expecting and *Teenage Pregnancies and Adoptions.*

My lips pressed together, and I quickly rang them up. I tried to carry books on every side of the spectrum. Whether I agreed with the subject or not wasn't up to me. What was up to me was ensuring I presented every side of an argument with the selection I carried. Knowledge was power, but one-sided knowledge could be dangerous. Knowing as much as you could about something could only serve you in the long run, or at least I thought so. This was why making decisions based solely on perception was dangerous. I spooled my thoughts and judgments back into my head. It's possible these books were not for the girl who stood in front of me. From both of their expressions, that probably wasn't the case, but it was not up to me to judge.

I rattled off the total to the woman and she paid with her card. Wrapping the books carefully and tucking them into a bag, I handed them over to her. "Thanks for coming by today."

"Thank you," the woman said quietly. "Savannah. Let's go."

Savannah searched my face looking for something. Judgment, perhaps?

It wasn't my place. We'd all done and said things we weren't proud of, and all of us had made mistakes we couldn't take back, some worse than others. I offered her a smile, and she ducked her head before following the woman out the door. I watched them walk away before I turned to Hardy.

"Dakota." He carefully set the book down. We stared at each other. His dark hair was a little too long these days, curling slightly over his collar. Those haunting blue eyes were the same, though there were a few more lines at the edges. Stress, no doubt. Our town had experienced an increase in crime that coincided with Hardy's arrival. It couldn't be easy for him.

"Hardy."

He took off his hat and sighed. "How are you?"

I wanted to tell him everything going on in my life. I wanted to invite him back to my home and make him pasta again. I wanted to cuddle with him on the couch.

I wanted...a lot. And he couldn't give me any of it. Not unless I changed who I was.

"I'm well," I said, shoving down the maelstrom of my thoughts. "How have you been?"

His lips thinned. Hardy looked up at the ceiling and snorted. "We're talking like we're strangers."

I didn't say a word. Perhaps we were strangers now. I wanted him as a friend even more than I wanted him as something more. At least now.

"I wanted to apologize."

I blinked. "Excuse me?"

He looked down. A muscle ticked in his jaw. "I haven't been kind to you over these last couple of months." Hardy sighed and lifted his head, meeting my gaze across the room. "It isn't easy always watching you throw yourself into harm's way for other people. That's my job."

Hardy was limited by the law. I was not. Therefore, I was unpredictable. "I'm...surprised."

A laugh escaped him. "I do my best to apologize when I'm wrong."

Could have fooled me. He'd been wrong several times. But this time, he'd been *really* wrong. I tilted my head and studied him. "So, what now?"

His eyebrows went up. "Well, usually when someone apologizes to you, the other person acknowledges it."

"I do acknowledge it. I'm just not sure how to respond yet."

Hardy's lips thinned. An exasperated sigh broke from him. "Dakota, I'm really trying here."

"You don't like who I am," I blurted.

His mouth fell open. "I don't know what–"

A scream tore through the morning, reverberating through the store. Hardy jerked and held up a finger. "Hold that thought." Without another word, he fled through the door and out into the street.

THREE

I, of course, followed him, though Hardy's legs were much longer, and I couldn't run as fast as him because of my love of pastries and hatred of exercise. But as it turned out, I didn't have far to run. Trudy stood outside her shop, her hands over her mouth. Her normally kind eyes were wide and frightened.

Hardy skidded to a stop in front of her. "What happened?"

She pointed wordlessly. He rushed into her restaurant, but this time I didn't follow.

"Trudy?" I held out my arms and gathered Trudy into a hug. Normally, she was the one who initiated, but today she needed it more than me. Her body shook as I held her. "It's okay," I said quietly. "Hardy will take care of whatever it is."

"There's nothing to take care of. She's dead."

I stiffened. "Who's dead?"

She stepped away from me and smoothed her hands down her flour dusted apron. "The girl I hired just a few weeks ago to help out at the shop."

"Tara?"

Trudy nodded. "I don't know how it happened. I was here the entire time, and I didn't hear a thing!"

"You saw her come in?"

She shook her head. "That's the thing. Tara wasn't due to work until noon."

Strange. "Where did you find her?"

Trudy's hand fluttered up to her neck. "The walk-in." She swallowed hard. "They're going to shut me down for a while. I know it."

Trudy had a lot of success lately. She had three shops open, all selling her baked goods and coffee creations, and it was only a matter of time before she opened more. There was even talk about franchising, though she'd pulled away from that some. We'd talked about it in depth before she made the decision, but it ultimately came down to her wanting to have some say over what's sold in the shops and that meant also being in control of the ingredients and the preparation methods. The outfit she'd been working with wasn't on board with it. I didn't think the deal had fallen apart yet, but maybe it had and Trudy just hadn't told me yet.

"We can work around it if it happens."

"*When* it happens," she said grimly.

She was right. It would happen. The place where she

stored many of her most important ingredients was contaminated now.

And wasn't that curious?

"I'll talk to Hardy and see if he can do anything to speed up getting you back into your kitchen." Just as I was about to step inside, Trudy tugged on my arm.

"There's something else you should know."

I paused at her tone. With wide and serious eyes, she leaned closer and whispered in my ear, "She was tied up just like the last book you gave me."

Chills ran down my spine. "The same way?"

Trudy nodded. "The exact same way. I didn't see what happened to her, but it was hard not to notice how she was left."

My throat clicked as I swallowed. "Alright," I managed. "Can you send me the name of the book again?"

"Sure." Trudy dug out her cell phone as I slipped into her shop.

Everything was quiet and I shoved away the fear trickling down my neck as I made my way to the back. By now Hardy would have called the police, so I had a minute or two at most to find out what I could before the place was swamped.

"Dakota."

I squeaked and spun around. Hardy stood over by the coffee machine, giving me a grim look.

"What are you doing?"

I rolled my eyes. "You know exactly what I'm doing."

He offered a short nod. "I was afraid of that." Hardy

stepped forward, pulling something from his belt loop as he did. I frowned and started to ask what he meant when he took my wrist and something cold and metal enclosed it.

I gasped as I held my wrist up. "You cuffed me?!"

Hardy led me out of the shop and back onto the street. "For trespassing on a crime scene." He reached over and clicked the other cuff onto a *Yield* sign.

"Are you kidding me?" I screeched.

Trudy watched with wide eyes. Seconds later, other shopkeepers ventured out of their stores just as two police cruisers tore around the corner. My face went flame red and I put all the vengeance I could into the glare I settled on Hardy. The infuriating man shrugged. "You're lucky I didn't arrest you."

My mouth fell open. "You uncuff me right this second or I swear I'll–"

Hardy stepped so close to me our noses almost touched. His breath smelled like mint and his eyes were the color of a bright summer sky. "You'll what?"

My mouth clamped shut. Anger burned bright within me. "This would never work," I grit out.

His eyes shuttered. "You're right. I really hope it works out with your reclusive billionaire," he snapped right before he turned and went back into the shop.

Trudy whistled low.

"I'm allowed to see whoever I want whenever I want!" I shouted back at him, tugging at the handcuff only for it to clank and scrape against the sign. "I'm going to murder him," I muttered.

Trudy sidled up beside me. "I wouldn't say that too loud out here," she muttered, watching Clarke and a police officer I'd never seen before getting out of their cars and step onto the sidewalk.

Her name tag read Short, and she was gorgeous. Diminutive and curvy, with long blonde hair captured in a snug bun, she gave me a long look before brushing right past me. Clarke dipped his head and followed after her.

"She's stunning," Trudy remarked but withered when I turned my glare on her.

"What? I've never seen her before," she said defensively.

The green-eyed monster reared its ugly head inside of me. Ugh. I had no business being jealous of a woman I didn't know for a man who'd just handcuffed me to a pole. What was *wrong* with me?

A familiar car turned the corner and I sagged against the pole in embarrassment. "Great," I muttered.

A choked laugh burst from my friend. "Oh goodness."

Was it possible to die of humiliation? I was about to find out. The car pulled into a spot right in front of my shop and two older women got out. A trim, athletic woman with chin-length red hair and another skinny one with steel gray hair and enormous Coke-bottle glasses.

Grandma and Aunt Corky.

Grandma was sassy, but she knew when to hold her tongue. All I got from her was a raised eyebrow. Aunt Corky wouldn't recognize tact if it smacked her in the face.

She peered closer; her eyes magnified at least four

times in those enormous glasses and cackled. "Never took you for an exhibitionist!"

"Corky!" my grandmother admonished.

Trudy pressed her lips together and turned away. I was glad she found amusement after what she'd stumbled on, but not so glad it came at my expense.

"Oh hush, Charlotte. You gotta admit she looks positively ruffled hanging onto that pole like one of those women from that boom boom club your daddy used to go to."

Trudy sounded like a tire deflating.

"Aunt Corky," I groaned. "Can you not?"

My grandmother sighed and pushed ahead of Corky. "You okay, honey?" She bent down and peered at the handcuff and back up at me with a questioning look in her eyes.

"Hardy did it."

One of her eyebrows rose. "For fun?"

My friend cackled like a witch on Halloween. I shot a glare at her. "No, Gran. He accused me of trespassing."

"She *was* trespassing." The traitor stood right outside of my vision. Gran looked him up and down. She tended to be a matchmaker, but even she probably wouldn't be keen on her granddaughter being handcuffed in broad daylight.

"Are you *trying* to get her to hate you, young man? If you are, you're doing a fine job."

Hardy stepped into my eyeline. "No, ma'am. But she can't just go traipsing all over a crime scene."

Gran looked around. "I don't see any crime tape. Or

ambulances." She looked up at the sky as if a plane was flying past announcing we were at a crime scene.

Color crept up Hardy's neck. "Ma'am, I assure you—"

"The police are here, but I don't see anything denoting a crime was committed here. Perhaps Dakota innocently followed you in to tell you something that she and Trudy spoke about." Gran's shrewd gaze found Trudy's. "Isn't that right?"

Trudy didn't know Gran well, but everyone took the woman seriously. Maybe it was her steely-eyed gaze when she asked you a question or her rod straight spine. I'd never seen the woman slouch. "Yes, Ms. Adair," Trudy said. "I remembered something after you left."

Hardy's eyes narrowed.

Gran turned to my current nemesis. "I suggest you uncuff my granddaughter in the next ten seconds or the next place you'll see me is in your supervisor's office."

I clicked my jaw shut and ducked my head.

Seconds later, the cuffs fell away and Hardy disappeared back into *Sprinkle Heaven* without a word.

"Well," Gran said. "Want to bring me up to speed on what that was all about?" She watched the back of Hardy until he rounded the corner of the shop. "I expect this little incident will further delay your mother her grandchildren?"

I groaned.

When I didn't respond, Gran harrumphed. "I suppose from what I just witnessed you and Hardy are no longer tiptoeing around each other sniffing for any dating potential?"

"Gran." Exasperated, I rubbed my wrists and sent a pleading look to Trudy for help. She gave me a slight shake of her head and stepped away.

"Traitor," I muttered.

"I should have known when I didn't hear anything at bridge night. You two used to be a hot topic of conversation. What happened, dear?" Gran reached over and brushed a lock of hair that had fallen in my face. Then she held onto my chin and forced me to look at her. "The truth and not some wild tale you tell your mother to placate her."

I sighed and extricated myself from her grip. "He doesn't like who I am."

Gran's eyes widened. "How can anyone not like you?"

A laugh escaped me. "You're biased, Gran. He doesn't like me getting involved in his cases."

Corky snorted at that. "Then he should get better at solving them."

"I heard that!" Hardy shouted at us.

The man had ears like a cartoon character.

"Hardy is good at his job, but there are things he can't get involved with legally. It's a lot trickier for him than it is for me." Hardy had a couple of valid points, and he was right that most of the time I plowed headfirst into danger without any sense of self preservation. I swallowed hard and looked away.

Gran touched my shoulder. "Never apologize for who you are. People who care about you will always be concerned when you put yourself in danger, but you're one of the few who would. Most people would walk away." She squeezed and brought me in for a hug, enveloping me in a vanilla scented hug. "I have to run. Corky and I have yoga in an hour and we're going to have to find a new shop for tea." She gave Trudy a regretful look. "I hope this is all resolved quickly." Gran pulled a twenty from her purse and handed it to her. "Keep this as a raincheck and save us two dirty chai's for next time?"

Trudy took the proffered bill and nodded. "Sure thing, Ms. Adair."

Gran winked at her. "Call me, Gran, darling."

She and Corky breezed away and climbed back into their car. I watched them speed away, intent on their search for another place to get pre-yoga tea.

"Your Grandma is awesome."

"She is," I mused.

"Ms. Corky, too."

"She's a handful." Shaking my head, I rubbed my wrists one more time. "I have to get back to the store, but if you need anything pop over or call, okay?"

Trudy looked longingly at her store. "I will." A sigh raised her shoulders and she leaned against the brick wall. "Hopefully Hardy won't be too long."

He walked out, carefully not looking at either of us, carrying a handful of crime scene tape. I rolled my eyes. "See you," I said to Trudy and headed back over to my shop.

I needed to put up a *No Hardy* sign in the window before he popped back over to yell at me again.

FOUR

It took the better part of two hours for the police to clear Trudy's shop. I did my best not to keep glancing out the window for a glance at Hardy and when I couldn't resist, I noticed Hardy doing his best not to look at my shop.

Trudy had messaged me the name of the book quite a while ago. I didn't have a current copy of *The Murder Code*, but I called up Harriet over in Candlelight Springs to see if she had an extra. Harriet owned Binders, a competing bookshop in the next town, but after getting to know her, I no longer thought of her as a competitor. She was slowly becoming a friend and we chatted at least once a week about upcoming releases. Harriet taught me how to up my window display game, and sometimes we boosted each other's inventory based upon the trends in our respective areas.

"I have two extra copies," Harriet said. "Want me to put one aside?"

"Please. I'll come by right after I close the shop. You going to be there around 5:30?"

Harriet laughed. "Of course, I will. It's been busier than usual, so I haven't been leaving the shop until seven most nights."

"Great." I peered up at the digital clock on the wall. "I'll close a little early and head on over."

She must have heard something in my voice. "Everything okay?"

"You'll hear about it sooner than later. Trudy found a body in her walk-in."

Harriet gasped audibly. "What is with these two towns lately?" She sighed. "Heaven forbid. It feels like we've become the murder capital of the state!"

"It is pretty strange," I admitted. "The poor girl was someone Trudy had just hired a couple of weeks ago, but what's even stranger is the murder appears to be a copycat of one in the book I need."

"I read this one a couple of weeks ago. Super creepy," she admitted. "Which one?"

"I don't really know. Trudy said something about the way they tied her up."

"Oh goodness," Harriet murmured. "I'll mark the page for you, darling. If you have time, come a little earlier and we'll have a cup of coffee if you have time."

"I always have time for coffee." The bell over the door rang. A man and a woman walked in. Tourists, obviously. People didn't dress up like those two around here. "I have to run. See you later tonight?"

"You have a date," Harriet said. "I'll have the book for you tucked under the register."

"Thanks, Harriet," I said and disconnected.

The couple walked in and beelined straight for the crime fiction without even saying hello. Not uncommon with tourists depending on where they came from. I noticed people from the east coast were a little less friendly initially than southern folks were, but they warmed up pretty quickly once you started chatting. I left them to their own devices and Googled the author and the book.

Jeff Martins had only written two books, but he'd been involved in crime his entire life. As a retired homicide detective, he was exposed to horrific crimes on an almost daily basis. I grimaced as I read through his bio. He'd started as a beat cop and slowly worked his way up to Homicide. The case that made him was that of a serial killer two states over who had murdered twenty women across the country. Jeff had figured out the killer was a long-distance truck driver and had slowly stalked him over the years, mapping out his routes and where he'd dumped his bodies. When the cycle started over, he was able to nab him. When the trial started, it came out that the man was responsible for much more than twenty deaths. By the time it was over, fifty families received closure and they sentenced the killer to two consecutive life terms with no chance of parole.

I shivered and clicked off his website. I liked a good mystery book like the next person, but his books might go a little too far for me. I liked my crime a little more on the cozy side and less on the violent side. I enjoyed his first book, but I hadn't started the one Trudy had read and now I wasn't sure I ever would.

A couple of minutes later, the couple headed up to the desk with three different books, one of them by Jeff Martins. "I enjoyed this one," I said as I rang them up. "I'm out of the copies of his newest book, but I heard it was good."

The husband looked like a studious sort. "I read it before this one. It was good but a little too much for me."

Ha. Same thing I was just thinking.

"I don't like books that keep me up at night."

His wife gave him an indulgent smile. "I'm the one who likes the scary books." She tapped the second selection; a book called *No Time to Kill*. "This one is amazing. Have you read it?"

I shook my head. "My TBR pile is embarrassing." I waved a hand around the store. "Can you imagine standing in one every single day?"

The woman laughed. "It would be a dream." She hooked a thumb at her husband. "He's already pretty patient about my reading habits. I can't imagine what he'd do if I owned a bookstore."

Her husband shrugged. "Probably cook my own dinner every night."

She snorted and swatted him. "Burn your dinner most likely."

He tugged her closer and kissed her on top of the head. "She's right," he admitted sheepishly.

My heart warmed at their camaraderie. "How long are you in town?"

"At least a week," the husband said. "Though we are a little concerned about what's going on next door." I glanced outside only to see two more police cruisers outside the window and more personnel milling around Trudy's shop.

"The police have it under control. I don't think there's anything to worry about." I kept my voice steady while I lied through my teeth. "Maybe something happened in the kitchen."

"We're up at the new B&B a few blocks over," the woman said. "It's quiet and the food is good, so even if we don't get out after today, it would still be a great vacation."

The husband paid with his card, and I pushed their purchase over to them. "There's an adorable little town not too far away if you're interested. They have a great coffee shop and another bookshop. I visit frequently so I'm a little bit biased."

"We might check it out," he said as he picked up the bag. "You ready?" he asked his wife.

"Let's get some lunch and get back for some reading."

"Don't forget the Valentine's Festival," I reminded them right before they walked out.

Hopefully we would still have it. Trudy normally took on quite a bit of the drink and dessert duties, but with the incident in her store, it might be a lot harder to access her supplies. She had two other stores, but it wouldn't be nearly as easy since this one was right in town where the festival was held.

I sent her a quick text asking how she was.

Everything is taped off. They won't let me access anything right now.

I'm sorry, I sent back. *Hopefully they'll find whoever it is and get things back to normal.*

Famous last words, Trudy texted.

The three little dots kept going and I waited, but they stopped and started a few times before they disappeared for good. Sighing, I put my phone down and stood up to straighten the store.

FIVE

I never put the *No Hardy* sign up, but I don't think it would have mattered. He strolled in right as I was poised to lock the door, not saying a word. Hardy brushed past me, leaving the scent of faint cologne and anger. I didn't bother to stifle my sigh. I turned the lock so no one else would come in and leaned against the door, arms crossed over my chest.

If we were in a western, this would be a standoff. Tension crackled in the air between us.

"This needs to stop," Hardy said.

"This?"

He waved a hand around in frustration. "This anger we have between us. Whatever this is."

"Hardy, the only anger I have is not being accepted."

He ran two hands through his hair, leaving it standing straight up. I chewed my lip to keep from laughing because he looked like he was about to scream. "I accept you just fine!" His face went red, and he scrubbed a hand over his chin as he turned away. "I just don't want you at my crime scenes!"

"Or in your investigations. Or anywhere near you and your job."

He spun back around. "Yes! You are not a police officer."

"We've established this many times. I'm a bookstore owner, so I should just stay in my lane?"

He nodded, relief sparking in his eyes. "Yes. That's it."

"Do one thing I'm good at and nothing else?"

He blinked. "Erm."

"Just stay here, filling out my inventory sheets, selling books to tourists and then go home each night without asking any questions?"

"Dakota," he growled.

"Just wait for my friends to get arrested and wait for them to get convicted?" That statement was probably a tad overdramatic, but my annoyance at him wouldn't go away.

"That isn't what I'm saying. You have to trust me."

"But you don't have to trust me?"

He took a step forward. "I do trust you. I just don't–"

A knock on the door startled me.

Hardy's face went tight, and his jaw clenched.

"Dakota?"

Daniel Jensen's voice came through the door. I squeezed my eyes shut for a brief moment before I turned and unlocked it. He breezed through carrying a bottle of wine and a bag from a great cheesesteak place down the road. It didn't matter what Daniel ate. He always had to pair it with a good wine. The smell wafted up from the bag, and I inhaled for a second.

"Everything okay?" he asked, his gaze flicking from me to Hardy.

"Perfect," I said. "Hardy was just leaving."

I eyed him. Hardy opened his mouth to say something before he snapped it shut and stalked past us, throwing the door open so hard the bells jangled together in a harsh cacophony.

I watched him all the way until he made it to his cruiser. When he slid in, our eyes locked, but neither of us gave anything away.

"So..." Daniel drawled. "That seemed intense."

"He's angry at me."

Daniel snorted. "Again?"

I had to laugh. "Again." I took the bag from him and walked over to the seating area. "I'm supposed to go to Harriet's this evening, but I have time for a bite."

"Good. Sorry to show up unannounced like this, but I had to come into town to pick something up from the tailor's and thought I'd grab dinner to go." He uncorked the bottle of wine and poured us both a glass in the two collapsible cups he carried with him. I asked him about it once and he told me that thirst waits for no man. I thought it was good that he stayed so hydrated, but I had yet to see him use the things for water. When I questioned him, he laughed and said, "Wine and water are two different kinds of thirst. I can get water anywhere, but wine is an experience." Whatever that meant.

We sat opposite each other and as Daniel was passing over one of the boxes, I remembered yesterday's awkwardness. Color flooded my cheeks, but Daniel passed over one of the cups without a word. We dug in and he chatted inanely about everything except for what happened. When I was halfway finished, Daniel cleared his throat.

"I'm assuming you somehow managed to get yourself involved in another case. Is that why Hardy was here and so angry?"

The cheesesteak turned into a lump in my stomach. "I'm not involved in anything," I insisted. "One of Trudy's employees was killed earlier today or sometime last night. She found her in the walk-in."

Daniel grimaced. "Let me guess. You were here when it happened?"

I eyed him. His tone was level, but his words made me bristle. "I was in my store, yes. We're right next door to each other."

"Hardy almost flew out of here on a rage broom."

The image made me chuckle. "He flies that rage broom around me a lot. I swear I haven't gotten involved."

He eyed me over the top of his flimsy cup. "And if she asks you?"

My lips twisted. "If she asks, I would. She's my best friend in town, Daniel. How could I say no to her?"

A sad smile turned his lips down. "You open your mouth and say no." He shrugged. "I don't agree with

Hardy," he added quickly when he noticed the thunderous frown forming on my face. "But I do worry about you. You've been lucky so far."

"Not you, too," I muttered under my breath.

Daniel reached over and touched my hand. "Dakota, listen to me. You have to realize he has a point. Interfering in an investigation could have serious consequences for a case when it goes to trial."

I set my sandwich down, suddenly not hungry anymore. "Why the sudden change of heart?"

"There was no change of heart. I enjoy your company, but it's nerve-racking to hear about all of the things happening around here." He took a sip of his wine. "I will never treat you like Hardy, Dakota. I promise. But I do think you should weigh the consequences of continuing to get involved."

I stood and crumpled up the sandwich papers, tucking everything back into the bag. "I'll keep that under advisement, but if you'll excuse me, I need to go meet Harriet and I'll be late if I dally any longer." My purse was underneath the register, so I hurried over to get it and pulled out a twenty-dollar bill.

Daniel frowned at it.

"Thanks for dinner." I tossed the bill down on the table between us and dug my keys out of my pocket.

He stared up at me for a long moment. "You're angry."

"I'm not." This wasn't a lie. What I was, though, was tired of people telling me what to do.

"Then why are you practically picking me up by the

seat of my pants and tossing me out of your store?" Daniel gathered up the remnants of our interrupted dinner and corked the bottle of wine. I took the two cups and tossed the rest down the sink before rinsing them and handing them back.

"I told you I have a prior engagement."

"Ah," Daniel said. "I suppose it will be a while before I hear from you, then?"

"My vacation is over, so I can't play chess as much as I have been." I looked at the floor so he couldn't see the lie in my eyes. I had no kids, no pets, and nothing much to do once I got off work. We both knew it, too. Steeling myself for an argument, I looked up only to see hurt flickering in his gaze. Daniel stood with the bag and the bottle. "Very well then. I'll see myself out."

I walked him to the door, but Daniel turned, putting us too close. I tilted my head up at him, only to see the intensity of his gaze. Swallowing hard, I tried to step away, but he snagged an arm around my waist. "Caring about someone is not suppressing them, Dakota. I merely wanted to say my piece. If you choose to keep getting involved, that is none of my business, and I will endeavor not to make it mine. I only wanted you to know how I felt about it."

My fingertips rested lightly against his chest. "Okay," I said breathlessly.

"We are not only friends." A lock of dark hair fell over his eyes. "Even if you don't want to admit it." A smile quirked one side of his mouth. "Friends do not run almost screaming out of someone's house when the subject of dating comes up. They talk about it." He stroked a hand down my arm and my mouth went dry. "Think about it, Dakota. I'll never try to turn you into someone else, but it will be difficult for me to watch you run headfirst into danger."

He grinned at me then and released me. "In fact, I won't do it."

I inhaled an angry gasp, but Daniel tapped me on the nose. "I'll run headfirst with you before I watch you do it alone."

And just like that, the bubble of anger I'd wrapped myself in popped. I blinked up at him, unsure what to say.

"Goodnight, my more than friend," Daniel said and stepped through the door without another word.

I watched until he drove away and then a strangled scream tore from my throat.

Men. Why were they so handsome and yet so frustrating?! And why did Daniel Jensen speak like a poet?!

I thunked my head against the thick glass of my shop door and stayed that way until the frigid glass cooled my heated face.

SIX

Cole caught me just before I got to my car. A relieved expression crossed his face when he stopped a few feet away.

"Dakota! I'm so glad I caught you." I hadn't seen him for a couple of weeks now. He'd been pretty busy at work and with his current girlfriend. I missed the camaraderie we once had, but that was life, wasn't it? We all got busy, formed new relationships, and in some ways moved on from the older ones.

"Everything okay?" I plopped my purse on the hood and leaned against it, dying for the chance to take my shoes off and rest a while. The weather was still frigid, but it would warm up in the next month or so. Right now, I wished I had a warmer jacket.

"I got caught up at work today, so I never got the chance to check in with you. We have a few people working on the *Sprinkle Heaven* story, but one of our guys said they saw you..." he paused.

"Handcuffed to a pole?" I added dryly.

Cole's brow furrowed, but his green eyes sparked with interest. "Yes. What was that about?"

"Hardy," I said. Cole knew how Hardy felt about me getting involved with his cases.

Surprise lit his face. "Hardy was the one who handcuffed you?"

"Yup."

He chuckled.

"Not funny, Cole," I groused.

"A little funny." He took a few steps toward me and pulled me in for a hug. I rested my cheek against his chest. "Are you okay?"

"I'm fine. Just embarrassed."

He let go and stepped back. "I've already made them promise not to put that part in the story."

Relief speared me. "Thank you."

"But really, why did he handcuff you?"

"I tried to step into the crime scene."

Cole shook his head. "Seriously? You're lucky he didn't arrest you."

"He could have tried," I grumbled.

"Regardless, I'm glad you're okay. How's Trudy holding up?" Cole and I almost fell out over him using our relationship as a way to get information on his stories. I was glad to say, he was mostly over that. I occasionally still saw the old journalist gleam in his eye, but he did his best to save that for other people and not me.

"As well as can be expected. The girl was a new hire."

"I heard. Do they have any leads?"

One of my eyebrows went up. Cole raised his hands in surrender. "Off the record. I'm only asking as a friend and as someone who's desperate for one of her lattes every morning. If she's not able to open, I may need to drive to the next town over for my caffeine fix."

"Or you could just pop into the store and get a cup there."

Cole held a hand over his heart. "As generous as that offer is, your coffee is not a latte and you do not possess Trudy's magical coffee skills."

"You're right," I admitted. "Maybe I'll lose a few pounds before this is over."

Cole grinned. "But do you really want to?"

Slinging my purse back over my shoulder, I opened my car door. "In lieu of missing Trudy's treats?" I rolled my eyes heavenward. "Never."

He tapped the hood of my car. "Then we better hope this is over as soon as possible otherwise we'll all be in caffeine withdrawal and that won't be good for anyone."

I wiggled my fingers at him. "Don't be a stranger. Pop by the shop on Friday. I should have that book you ordered with the morning deliveries."

His eyes lit up. "I'll be in first thing!"

Cole jogged away and I headed out of town and toward Candlelight Springs. I'd rather be in my jammies with a cup of cocoa, but I needed that book and had promised her I'd be by tonight.

I'D LEARNED window display art from the best, but so far this student had not surpassed the master. The green-eyed monster hit me as I ventured up to Binders' front door and saw what Harriet had done.

February was traditionally known as the month of love, but there were several high-profile crime fiction releases right around Valentine's Day this year. Harriet had combined the best of both worlds. She'd made a banner out of yellow crime scene tape and strung little foil hearts all over it. Hanging off the center was a small sign that said, "Love got you down? Try a little murder instead."

I slapped a hand over my mouth to keep from laughing out loud. Hardy would be appalled. She'd added little chalk body outlines on the floor of the window scene but interspersed a Valentine's theme throughout. There was a small chocolate cake and a bottle of wine on a small table, set up with two chairs and a small, wrapped gift box. Next to that was a green glass bottle with a poison label on it, tipped over on its side with chartreuse liquid dripped around it and on the bottle and plates.

To the right of it were several popular thriller selections and one rom-com with a clumsy private investigator who was notoriously terrible at relationships. I wish I'd thought this up. As it was, I hadn't even bothered to set mine up yet.

Harriet saw me through the window and waved. I headed inside and straight over to the register. Two customers were in front of me, but Harriet motioned for me to wait for her in the cute little seating area she'd arranged in the spirit of the holiday.

Valentine's Day had never been my favorite. I always thought it was too commercialized, and the last thing I'd rather do is wait an hour in a crowded restaurant for fishy crab cakes and a bottle of wine four times the cost of what I could buy it for at the grocery store. But to each his own. Harriet appeared to love it to the extreme. I looked up only to see red and silver streamers covered in tiny hearts strung all throughout the store. Fortunately, she stopped there because if I had seen hanging naked Cupids, I would have staged an intervention.

When she finished, she brought over two cups of coffee. "Decaf," she said. "If I drank regular at this time, I'll be up all night."

I accepted it gratefully as Harriet sat down across from me. She pushed a small package over. "This is the book you needed, and I also downloaded and printed the discussion questions." Her brow crinkled. "You might find them interesting." Harriet took a sip of her coffee. "Now tell me, honey. Is Trudy okay?"

"She's okay. Shaken up and worried about what comes next with her store, but she's holding up better than I might have."

Harriet laughed. "I doubt that, but I'm glad she's doing

okay. That poor girl," she mused. "I wonder what happened."

"I can't say. Trudy didn't know her all that well. She was a new hire from what I understand, brought on to help her manage the workload the other two storefronts placed on her."

"She refused franchising?"

I nodded. "For now."

Harriet tsked. "I know she likes to have control of her brand, but franchising might have taken at least some of the workload from her."

"She might change her mind later." I doubted it, but maybe this would change her mind, as unfortunate as it was.

"Maybe so," she mused. "So tell me, how was your vacation?" Her eyes sparkled. "We don't have quite the rumor mill your town does, but I've heard a few people remarking about a pretty dark-haired woman visiting with the town's favorite author."

A blush stole over my cheeks. "We're only friends." Daniel's words fluttered through my mind. More than friends. Maybe we were. I still didn't know how to feel about the strange turns my life had taken over the last year or so, but this is the hand I'd been dealt, and having two handsome men circling around me wasn't as bad as it could be. I just wished Hardy yelled a lot less.

"Mmm hmm," Harriet said, but I could tell she wasn't buying it. "And what about that yummy detective?"

"If Hardy doesn't stay away from me, I'm bound to

cause him a heart attack. He looks like he's close to bursting a blood vessel every time he's around me."

"I'm sure he won't mind if he has a heart attack over you." The tone belied her words and we both laughed. No one wanted a heart attack, but maybe Hardy would leave me alone if he was laid up in the hospital for a while.

Uncharitable, but I sure could use another break. Even though I'd just had one. Harriet tapped the package. "If you open it, I'll show you what I'm talking about."

I slipped the book out of the bag and noticed several brightly colored flags marking pages. Harriet touched a blue one. "This is the scene I think your friend is talking about."

I flipped to it and skimmed the page, grimacing the further I read. "Oof."

Harriet murmured her agreement. "I think someone might be a fan of this author or since he's a former detective, maybe it's someone he's put away." Her voice lilted in a question. I hadn't thought of it that way, but maybe she was right.

"Hmm. I wonder how we can find out what cases he's worked on?"

Harriet sipped her coffee. "I don't think there's an official way to get them, but you might be able to search news articles. A lot of reporters will name the investigating detectives. You might not be able to get all of them, but I bet you could find most."

"That's a great idea." I flipped through the rest of the tabs. "What are the others for?"

She shrugged. "Just interesting tidbits I thought might help. I enjoyed this book but found it far too creepy to read anything else he's written. This appeals to people who read hard core thrillers. I'm not one of those. I like my thrillers a little warmer. Like on the beach. With a clumsy amateur investigator." Harriet laughed. "Like Stephanie Plum or the other one I can't remember. *Body Movers* or something."

"I love both of those." We sat in silence for a few. "Poor Trudy."

Harriet made a humming noise. "You don't think this has anything to do with her, does it?"

"What do you mean?"

"She's been involved in the last couple of cases. It seems odd for someone who's merely a shop owner to have two back-to-back crimes she's been directly involved in, don't you think?"

"It does seem odd," I admitted. "Maybe someone doesn't want her to succeed?"

"Can you think of anyone she might have angered?"

I shook my head. "I'm not sure. It's difficult to get a shop up and running in Silverwood. It's a small town and people tend to stay loyal to the places that came before it. Sometimes I think the only reason I've had such luck is I bought the place from a local. Since it came with the cat, maybe it was an easier transition than trying to build something from the ground up."

"Or you have an amazing store and an amazing personality and people respond to that?"

I gave her a grateful look. "I think you're too kind to me." Setting my coffee cup down, I crossed my legs and peered at her. "Also, I have to tell you I am super jealous of that window display. How in the world are you that creative?"

Harriet chuckled and glanced over to the display. "I have a notepad in the shower."

I burst out laughing.

She held her hands up. "I'm serious! I put a lot of things on it. My grocery list. Anything I think I might forget if I don't write it down right then and any ideas I have for the displays. Sometimes I think I forget more than I remember. My mind feels like a sieve these days."

"I know what you mean. All I have is a pile of ribbon scattered in the window. With the festival just a few days away, I really need to get it done, but I can't seem to concentrate. I still have vacation brain, I think."

"You needed it." Harriet stood. "Want some more coffee?"

"Thanks, but no. I need to get home. Poppy has been there all day and if she doesn't eat by a certain time, I may come home to shredded curtains." I picked up my purse. "Thanks for this," I said, holding up the book. "I'll take a look at everything you marked."

"Best of luck."

I rolled my eyes. "I don't need luck because I'm not getting involved!"

"Famous last words," Harriet said as she walked me to the door. "We always know how that ends."

Harriet was right, though. I always said this, so why shouldn't I just embrace it? After all, Hardy and I arguing over it all the time always ended with me defending myself. I clutched the book tighter to my chest and hurried to the car.

Embrace it.

Maybe I would.

SEVEN

Poppy paced by her food bowl, giving me a baleful look when I rushed in and dropped my keys on the kitchen counter.

"Sorry! Sorry!" I said as I rushed over to the food canister. Poppy was nothing if not punctual. If there was no food in her bowl by 7:30, heaven help the furniture. I learned this the hard way when she first came home with me. She was a cat driven by her belly and she had particular tastes in food, too. Salmon or chicken. No beef. Beef would result in her parking herself by her food bowl and making a ruckus.

I poured in a couple of scoops of dry food and moistened it with just a touch of the wet food she liked. She didn't wait for me to finish and nudged my foot when she attacked her dinner.

Speaking of which, I had no idea what I would eat. The turn in conversation with Daniel had ruined my appetite then, but now I was hungrier than I thought I would be. The book rested on the kitchen counter waiting for me to a deep dive. I'd look at it after I'd eaten and see if I could come up with anything.

Twenty minutes later, I had a Caesar salad and a passable bowl of mushroom pesto pasta in front of me. The grocery store had a new delivery of fresh pastas, and I had neither the patience nor the knowledge to try to make fresh pasta, so I grabbed a mushroom and a cheese ravioli the other day. The pesto sauce was also jarred but fresh.

I brought the book and my plate to the living room and kicked off my shoes before I settled onto the couch. Poppy had long finished her dinner and had curled up on the recliner, purring contentedly in her sleep. I flipped on the television for background noise and cracked open the book to the first marker Harriet set.

Skimming through, I didn't see too much, only a physical description of the potential killer. What difference that made, I had no idea. Maybe Harriet thought the current killer would look similar? It seemed like a far reach to me, though I jotted it down into the small notebook I kept by the couch. I normally used it for grocery or reminder lists, but this case seemed more involved than the others I'd been involved in, at least on the surface. I'd transfer everything over to a new notebook later.

I ate and took notes for the next hour, wondering at the inner workings of Harriet's mind. Some of the marked pages I didn't understand. Other ones were crystal clear. So far, I had a potential description, some habits, the possible murder weapon and the exact way Tara had died. If it was exactly like the murder in the book. Frowning at my notes, I thought about what I was looking at and my conversation with Harriet.

If Jeff had been an investigator in the past, was it possible he based this current story on someone who actually existed? It seemed like a dangerous game of cat and mouse, but real life was stranger than fiction sometimes. If he had, who was it based on? I pushed my plate away and pulled my laptop toward me. Tapping on the table, I chewed my lip for a minute before I Googled the author's name and the words *homicide detective*. Over a hundred entries came up.

Jeff had worked in New York before he'd come to Virginia. I found it interesting he'd come from such a high crime area to an area like this one. He didn't live in Silverwood, but he wasn't too far away. He'd retired in Virginia and started writing not too long after. I clicked on the news stories one by one. Some weren't pertinent, but in others, I found interesting tidbits I'd jot down. He'd worked on numerous homicides, but so far, I hadn't found one similar to the one detailed in his book.

I found the serial killer case but couldn't read too much about it before I clicked off in disgust. Hopefully this wasn't linked. The culprit was rotting in prison now, thankfully, but some crimes were too much for me to swallow.

Just before I clicked my computer shut, I opened another news story I didn't think would add anything. As I skimmed, though, I ran across a note that said Jeff was being stalked and had to take out a *Temporary Restraining Order* on someone named Martin. There was no picture or last name.

I groaned in annoyance. Of course there wasn't. I tried to Google Jeff and Martin's names together, but nothing came up. I sat back and wondered if there was anything I could do.

A few moments later, an idea came to me. I grinned.

It had the potential to work perfectly.

THE NEXT MORNING, I unlocked the door to Tattered Pages and went straight to my computer. Jeff had to have an agent or publicist. If I could get him in the store, maybe I could ask him some questions about his prior casework, without uncovering what I was doing.

A few minutes later, I had the name of his agent, so I sent her a note. Jeff might be too big to frequent my bookstore for a signing, but if I could make it worth his while, maybe I could convince him to stop on his upcoming tour. The book was a new release, so hopefully I made it in time to see if they could slide me in.

A knock on the glass sounded just as I shut my computer. Trudy stood outside, holding two steaming cups. I hoped they were coffee.

Waving at her, I hopped out of my seat and unlocked the door for her. She breezed in, handing me one of the cups. "Americano. Hope you don't mind. I'm low on supplies and have to work with what I have."

"Please don't apologize. You're a wizard with anything involving coffee and milk." I held it up to my nose and inhaled. "I have some sugar if you want it."

"Yes, please." Trudy headed over to doctor up her coffee with me right behind her. When we finished, she settled into one of the chairs. Looking at her, I noticed fine lines of exhaustion beside her eyes. Her hair was in a messy bun and her clothes were wrinkled. "I must look a mess," she said with a sigh.

"Not at all. Long night?"

She nodded and leaned back in the chair, tilting her face up to the ceiling. "You would not believe the amount of questions Hardy had for me. I barely knew the girl and she didn't talk all that much anyway." Trudy sighed and straightened. "It's odd. Sometimes I have employees who come in and spill their guts about everything and sometimes they're tight-lipped and private. Figures the one time I needed someone to talk is the one time I got a quiet one." She shook her head. "I couldn't answer anything. I don't know if she has family close. I don't know if she was a student or if she was married. I didn't see a ring, but I don't allow anyone to operate the machine with one on. Maybe there's a husband out there who is wondering why his wife didn't come home last night."

I reached over and squeezed her hand. "Don't beat yourself up. It isn't your fault."

"Hardy mentioned you," Trudy added casually.

I stiffened. "Let me guess. He told you not to ask me for help?"

She snickered and took a sip. "That's exactly what he said, but he also asked me about what you were like as a business neighbor."

My brow furrowed in a frown. "That's odd."

"I thought so, too, but he wouldn't divulge the reason he was asking. Maybe there's someone angry that I'm expanding."

I peered at her. "Has something happened?"

"Not that I can think of. I haven't had a cross word with anyone in a long time. It's strange, though. We always have those customers who come in and think they know best, but they're almost always tourists." She rolled her eyes. "But there's never been a time where I thought someone would come back and try to ruin me. It's usually someone in a hurry and not used to the slow pace around here."

"What about at your other stores? Has there been anyone angry there?"

Trudy fell silent while she thought about it. "I don't think so. I had one incident with someone I was thinking about hiring as a store manager, but nothing came of it."

I pulled out my notepad and pretended not to notice Trudy's grin. "Tell me about that."

"You know, honey, I know you love your books, but maybe you should think about adding in some private investigating services. You're good at it."

"I think I get lucky more often than not."

Trudy tsked and shook her head. "You have to stop saying that. It's more than luck. Maybe it's because you're a reader. You're able to put one and four together even when it equals seven. Too many people think in a linear way. You're more like one of those crime boards with those strings pointing at every location in the city."

"I like it," I admitted. "Every crime is a puzzle that has to be solved. You just have to figure out the right direction the pieces are supposed to go in."

Trudy nodded. "Everything that has happened around here has had a strange seven degrees to Kevin Bacon vibe to it."

I snorted but when I thought about it, I realized she was right. "Maybe there's something bigger we aren't seeing here."

Trudy looked disturbed. "Maybe so. I hope digging deeper won't uncover something we don't want to see."

I shuddered. "There's no way to shove Pandora back into the box, though."

"Wouldn't it be something if she was cooperative?" Trudy mused.

We sipped our latte in companionable silence for a little while until there was another knock on the door. I looked at the clock and frowned. "I'm not open for another half hour," I groused.

Trudy's brows lifted. "I don't think he cares," she murmured.

I turned only to see Hardy's broad frame filling the doorway. A sigh escaped me before I could stop it, making

Trudy laugh. "I'll just take my coffee and go," she said in a singsong voice.

"Not so fast. Maybe he's here to see you."

Trudy grinned so wide, her eyes crinkled. "He's never here to see me, darling. But keep telling yourself that."

I shooed her toward the front, and she waved at Hardy as she slipped out. He caught the door before it shut and paused.

"May I come in?"

"Are you here in an official capacity?" I asked.

"I'm not on duty for another hour."

I frowned at him. "That didn't answer my question."

He held up a bag with a grease stain on the front. "I bring a peace offering."

The bag was from Silverwood's newest business, a donut place called Do Nut Pass Go. They made the best apple fritters on the planet. Almost drooling, I snatched the bag from him and peered inside. I'd never told Hardy my favorite offering there, but it was a small town, and someone was bound to notice me going in almost every weekend. I thought about maybe wearing a disguise so I wouldn't seem like I needed an intervention.

Two apple fritters and a blueberry cake donut. I almost sighed in delight but managed to keep my face blank. Although the offering of donuts was a good one, I wasn't ready to forgive him yet. Waving Hardy back, I stopped at the small coffee area and poured him a cup. "Cream and sugar?"

"Black."

Like your soul, I almost said. I handed him the coffee and led him to the same area where Trudy and I were just sitting. "How's your morning?"

Hardy stared at me. "Fine," he said after a moment. "Yours?"

"Fine."

Silence stretched between us, and finally, I dug into the bag and started chowing down. It might be awkward between us, but it wasn't the donuts' fault, was it? Hardy never was a man who spoke a lot, but I wouldn't be the one to start this conversation. I'd come to the conclusion last night that I would no longer make excuses for myself. Making myself small only served other people, not me.

Hardy took out the blueberry donut, but at my look, he split it in half and put the other on top of the bag I was using as a plate. I halved the other apple fritter and pushed it over to him as a peace offering. We ate in tense silence for a few minutes.

"I'm sorry," he finally said.

"Okay."

Hardy looked down at the floor. "It's unacceptable to expect someone to change just because I don't like something about them."

I set the apple fritter down. "You are terrible at apologies," I said after a moment.

He shoved a hand through his hair. "I know."

He looked away from me, staring out the window at the cars passing by. "I grew up in a home where my father ruled. My mother stayed at home looking after me and my siblings."

I blinked. He rarely talked about his life. Sometimes it felt like his life was such a secret that he just sprung from the head of Zeus or something. "How many siblings do you have?"

"Three." Hardy took a sip of his coffee. "Two sisters and a brother."

"Do they live close?"

"No. They're across the country."

He set down his empty mug. I hurried to refill it, hoping he would keep talking.

"My mother wasn't allowed to work. Dad provided everything." His jaw clenched. "He saw the world as a dangerous place and acted like a protector for her." A sigh escaped. "It wasn't until I was older that I realized maybe Mom was in a prison she couldn't escape from."

"You can't protect everyone from everything."

"I know, but it's easier to think I can."

"It can't be easy doing the job you do and knowing it."

He thanked me for the coffee. "I...care about you."

"I know." I handed over the rest of the second fritter. "But I won't change for you."

"I know." He smiled, but it didn't touch his eyes. "I'd like to start over."

I wanted very much to do that, but we'd walked this path before.

"I'm serious."

"I won't change who I am or what I'm doing to be friends with you."

"I'm really trying, Dakota."

He sat there, his hands clenched on his lap, his eyes hopeful, and I relented. "Fine." I stuck my hand out. "I'm Dakota."

Hardy stared down for a moment before he took it in his own. I'd forgotten how warm and strong his hands were. "I'm Hardy."

"It's a pleasure to meet you."

Our gazes locked and warmth filled me. Seconds later, his eyes widened, and horror filled them.

"Dakota!"

Hardy launched himself across the couch.

EIGHT

The sound of shattering glass and the smell of smoke reached me first, even before the surprise of being tackled by Hardy. Then pain. Extreme pain.

A scream tore from me. Hardy lay on top of me for a brief second before he rolled off, scooped me in his arms and rushed me to the back of the store.

"Try not to move." His voice was low and urgent. Hardy laid me carefully across the couch in my office before he picked up the old rotary phone I kept in the back.

My eyes slowly began to shut as he rattled off who he was and what he needed from the dispatcher.

"Ms. Adair?"

My eyes blinked open, and I exhaled a pained breath as I shifted.

"Try not to move."

"Brody?"

The tall, handsome paramedic grinned down at me. "I wish I could say I'm surprised by this."

I snorted and shut my eyes. "My arm?"

"Broken, I'm afraid. I'm surprised you're not flattened like a pancake. Only the toughest people can take getting squashed by a giant detective."

My eyes widened as the memory came back. "Where is he?" I croaked.

"He said something about checking out your house." At my look, he shrugged. "No idea, Ms. Adair. He'll catch you up when he's back. In the meantime, we're going to need to transport you because that arm needs a cast."

"Noooo," I moaned.

"Oh yes. He landed right on top of you and your arm took the brunt of it. You'll be in one for at least a month." Brody adjusted the sling on my arm. "Let's just hope you aren't left-handed."

A thought occurred to me just then. "How am I going to read?"

The paramedic snickered. "My wife has this handy device that flips pages for her on her e-reader. Have you ever seen one?"

"Like a remote control?"

Brody tucked his tools of the trade into a case and snapped it shut. "Exactly like that. She's always complaining she has to stick one arm out of the covers when she's reading on her device so only one side of her gets frigid."

"That's genius," I marveled. "Do you know where she got it?"

"I'll ask and send a note to the store." He leaned over and held his hand out. "Here. I'll help you stand and get you out to the ambulance."

I balked. "I don't think a broken arm is worth an ambulance ride."

"You're on Tylenol and borrowed time, Ms. Adair. I strongly recommend you come with me."

"No thank you." I shook my head and stayed put. "It's way too expensive to take a ride with you. I'd rather drive myself than spend thousands on a five-minute drive."

Brody's lips thinned. "I understand, but I can't legally release you unless there's someone here to vouch for you. Whoever it is would have to take responsibility for you in case something happens."

"I'm a grown woman!"

"I'll take her."

Hardy stood in the doorway, his once pristine white shirt smudged with dirt and blood. There was a new cut on his cheek, red and angry in the dimmer light of my office. "Are you okay?" I breathed.

A muscle in his jaw ticked. "I'm better than you are." He came through the door and sat on the edge of the bed. "We need to talk in a minute." Hardy held his hand out to Brody. "Whatever you need me to sign, I will. Dakota and I will follow the ambulance back to the hospital."

Brody stared both of us down before he lifted a shoulder in defeat. "Fine." He opened his case back up and pulled out a few papers attached to a clipboard. "If anything happens to her, you'll be responsible for it."

"That hardly seems fair–" I began.

"You're safer with me than in an ambulance anyway," Hardy said as he scribbled his name on the forms and handed them back.

My mouth snapped shut. What in the world did that mean? "Is everything okay?"

Hardy's gaze lingered on Brody until the paramedic beat a hasty retreat. "Let me help you."

I swung my legs off the bed, hissing in pain as I jarred my arm. Hardy held his hand out. "Steady. If you can bear it, secure your arm with your other hand. I'll help you keep your balance. It will stop the arm from moving around too much."

Following his instructions, I let Hardy steady me and lead me out of the store. Glass lay littered on the floor. The table had blown over and snapped into several pieces. Coffee had spilled and stained the carpet. Donut remnants were sprinkled everywhere. "Oh," I breathed.

"I know. I'm so sorry," Hardy said, but he didn't allow me to linger. "I scheduled a company to come out later today. They'll patch it up for tonight and start work first thing tomorrow."

"I need to call the insurance."

He led me to his car and helped me slide in. "It's not necessary. The damage came from a current case, so the police department will cover the damages."

That didn't sound right. I waited until he slid into the driver's seat. "Hardy."

"Don't worry about it," he growled.

I fell silent. The town whipped past us as Hardy sped through the streets. He didn't say another word until he skidded the vehicle to a stop in front of the emergency room. My heart thudded slow and painfully. Whatever happened Hardy didn't want to tell me.

The detective jogged around to the passenger side, opened the door, and scooped me out.

"Hardy."

The doors slid open automatically and Hardy stormed through the ER entrance with me dangling in his arms like a princess rescued by her prince. I didn't know how to feel. Protected, yes. A little silly, too.

"Put me down," I whispered. Everyone, some of whom I knew, stared at us as he stalked past.

"No." His voice boomed against my ear. A sigh escaped me, and I turned my face into his chest. He cradled me in his arms, careful not to jostle me as best he could, and didn't even put me down when we reached the desk.

"She needs to see a doctor as soon as possible."

"There are many people ahead of you, sir."

I felt Hardy's heartbeat pick up. "Ms. Adair has been the victim of a crime and she's injured."

"I understand–"

"I'm afraid you don't." Something slapped down on the counter.

There was silence, then Brody's voice. "Detective Cavanaugh."

"Either she sees the doctor right now or—"

"Hardy." My fingertips pressed against his chest, and I tilted my head up. "It's just an arm."

His jaw clenched.

"Put me down."

"No," he said again.

"You have to when the doctor comes in," I said gently.

"When the doctor comes in," he repeated.

Brody's eyebrows went up a hair, and his gaze narrowed. Our eyes locked and naked curiosity shone there, but I just gave my head a tiny shake. Whatever this was, Hardy needed to hold me. So I would let him.

"Does she have insurance?" the woman asked.

"Yes," Hardy said.

"No," I said.

He stiffened and looked down. "You don't?"

"I'm a small business owner. Insurance is outrageous and I'm young and healthy."

"Bill me," Hardy told the woman.

"Absolutely not," I snapped.

"I'll put her down as self-pay for now," the woman said, her voice stretched to the limit of her patience.

"Can we sit?" I whispered.

She pushed over a pile of paper. I groaned at the sight of it. My arm throbbed in time with my heart.

"I'll do it," Hardy offered.

"You don't have to. Plus, you don't have any of my information."

Hardy walked with me over to the waiting area and sat on one of the couches, cradling me against his chest. "You can let me go now," I said quietly. My face burned as everyone stared openly.

"The doctor isn't here," he said matter-of-factly. He held the paper to the side of him and started filling out what he could, skipping over what he didn't know.

"Hardy, people are staring," I whispered.

"Let them."

"We aren't married."

His fingers stilled. "Does it matter?"

I was so red and hot I felt like I had a fever. "Well, I don't normally let men carry me through buildings like a princess."

"That isn't what I asked."

"This feels like we're more than friends," I mumbled.

"Then take it like that," Hardy said and continued to fill out my paperwork.

I gaped at him. "Hardy! An hour ago we weren't even friends!"

He set the pen down. "Twenty minutes ago, I drove past your house. Someone shattered your front windows and broke down your door."

Numbness filled me, but he kept talking. "I realized at that moment I want you in my life. I want you to be my friend. I want you to be more. And I know you want the same."

"This is madness," I muttered.

"This is life." He tilted my chin so that I looked at him. "We are different, but it no longer matters to me. I want you to be with me, Dakota. And if I have to marry you to get you to sit in my lap in public, then so be it."

"You don't mean that." I stared at Hardy, stunned.

"I do mean it. You make me insane with all your curious ways and your inability to worm yourself into everything I'm doing at work, but if something happened to you, my heart would break. I wouldn't want to live in this world without you."

Tears filled my eyes. "Hardy."

"Do not say a word until you have pain meds. Normally it's my head getting in the way of my heart, but I can see the wheels spinning in yours. We can work these differences out. At least I'm willing to try. Trying might mean letting go of some things in my life I've clung to, but that's what life is. Letting go of the things that no longer serve you."

"Dakota Adair?"

Hardy scooped me up again and walked me to the back of the hospital where he gently deposited me on an uncomfortable bed. My heart was full, but I was confused and leery and I didn't know if Hardy had been exposed to a toxic mold that made him way more reasonable and romantic than he ever had been.

I watched him through suspicious eyes even when the doctor tried to ask me questions. Hardy answered most of them. When he undid the makeshift sling and gently prodded me in the arm, I hissed and Hardy shot to his feet.

"Relax, Detective. I went to school for this."

Hardy glared at the doctor, but he remained unruffled. "We need to get an x-ray to see the extent of the break. From what I can tell, it's severe."

I started to look down, but the doctor shook his head. "I wouldn't."

"That bad?"

Sympathy filled his eyes. "Probably worse."

I grimaced but kept my eyes away from it. Hardy's face had gone pale as he looked down. "I did that," he said and closed his eyes. "I am so sorry."

"Better this than blindness or worse from flying glass," I said, trying to be flippant.

Hardy's face darkened. "I know what you're trying to do, but it's not helping."

"What's your pain level?" the doctor interrupted.

By now I was used to it. There was a slow, dull ache in it and if I moved it, my entire arm and collarbone burned like fire. "Six," I croaked out. "Maybe seven."

The doctor patted my knee. "I'll have a nurse come in with something stronger for you. The paramedics said they gave you Tylenol?"

I nodded.

"Give them about five or ten minutes." He nodded at Hardy and rose, leaving us alone in the room.

"What else happened?" I asked him.

He sat down at the edge of the bed. "There was a note."

"That doesn't sound as bad as your expression does right now."

Hardy's eyes shuttered. "Your house..."

I sat up straight. A scream tore from my throat as my arm jostled and tears streamed down my face. "Poppy! Where's Poppy!"

He touched my leg. "I dropped her at the police station. Don't worry. She's being fed lots of unhealthy things and being spoiled by Silverwood's finest."

"Is she okay?"

"She's uninjured but angry. I had a time trying to get her to come out especially when she realized you weren't there. I had to lure her in with tuna."

A smile quirked my lips. "Not surprising."

"I want you to move in with me."

I sputtered a choked cough. "Excuse me?"

Two nurses barged in pushing a large machine. "Excuse me, young man," one said to Hardy. He scooted out of their way and came over to the other side of the bed.

"We will talk about this later," I whisper-hissed.

"We will," he promised.

There was no way I was moving in with Hardy. What had gotten into him today?

NINE

I had to move in with Hardy. On the outside, the house looked fine. Nothing seemed out of place. The garden was still pristine, though right at the initial stage of needing to be weeded. I'd just had the yard mowed a few days ago and the edging still looked perfect. It wasn't until Hardy and I walked up the sidewalk that I noticed the front door.

"Oh," I breathed. Tears filled my eyes. The door hung askew, half in, half outside. Wood splinters scattered on the front porch and garden bed. But that wasn't all. Hardy held up the broken door and I slipped in.

"Be careful. There's a lot of–"

"Glass." I rubbed my face with my good hand and stared in horror at the remnants of my home. Hardy hovered at my back, his presence comforting me in the midst of this chaos.

"I haven't called the police yet. Once I do, you won't be able to come back in for a while. I thought you might want to get some clothing and any important documents you need."

"If they're still here."

"The front areas are the only ones that look disturbed. This was a warning."

I looked up at him. "A warning?"

He nodded toward the front window. The glass had shattered all over the couch and floor and the curtain rod hung askew on the wall. A large rock lay on top of my broken coffee table. Tied to it was a brown sheet of paper.

"Did you look at it?" I tiptoed around the broken glass of my possessions, past scattered paper, and shattered knick-knacks and bent down to untie the twine.

"I didn't. You should wait for the police, though."

I sighed as I struggled with one hand. "You are the police."

Hardy crouched down beside me. "I guess I am." He put his hands over my fingers. "At least put these on and try to salvage some evidence."

I took the latex gloves, slid them over my good hand and removed the paper from the rock. "I don't understand why they would throw a rock through my window and break in. It seems like overkill."

"I can't say. They probably came in first to see if you were home. This was probably done when they were leaving."

My heart thundered in my veins as I unfolded the paper.

Stay out of this, it read.

"Simple and to the point."

Hardy read over my shoulder. "He knows you." His knees cracked as he stood and pulled his phone out of his pocket.

"Who?"

"Whoever killed that girl knows who you are."

I swayed as I stood. There wasn't a single clean surface in the house. Every chair had shattered glass. Every surface was covered in dust or papers or liquid. I couldn't think about it too much because if I did, I would collapse.

"This is why you mentioned moving in."

Hardy held up a finger and rattled off my address and pertinent details to the operator. When he hung up, he pinched the space between his brows and leaned against the kitchen island. "I started it all wrong. Of course, I wouldn't expect you to move in with me. I have a guest house. It's furnished, has a kitchen, and a master bedroom. You can stay in it for as long as you need to."

"That's too much."

"You won't be able to stay here for a while. The police will be going in and out for a while and most of your furniture has been destroyed."

"Mom can help me with that. We have a lot of things in storage. I can stay with her." I didn't want to, but Mom would let me if I asked. She lived in a small one-bedroom apartment, similar to the one I used to live in. I'd just purchased the home a couple of months ago and home ownership was beginning to add up. I could pay off the mortgage, but I sure liked having that nest egg in my bank account.

"It's a guest house, Dakota. There's a kitchen and everything. You never even have to see me."

I eyed him. "You cavemanned me less than an hour ago and now you say I don't have to see you?"

Hardy pushed away from the island. "You were hurt, and I was responsible. I got a little...overprotective."

He laughed at my expression. "You don't have to answer anything we talked about except for this. You have your own entrance and exit, and it's been empty since I moved in. Just say yes, Dakota. Just until you get the place fixed."

I looked around at the destruction of my home, thought about what it would cost me to rent a hotel or B&B for the next few weeks and finally let out a sigh.

"Fine."

Hardy chuckled.

"Thank you," I grumbled.

"Good. Grab a bag as quickly as you can. The police will be here in a minute or two. The faster you can get your things, the faster we can get out of here."

Without another word, I left Hardy sitting in the ruins of my living room and hurried to the back to pack a suitcase.

WHEN I CAME OUT, the tiny blonde was standing in the middle of my living room and way too close to Hardy. I gave her a polite smile. She reached over and put her hand on Hardy's arm–a possessive gesture she punctuated with a smirking smile.

Considering I was standing in the ruins of my home, I didn't feel much like playing whatever game this was. "I'll be out at the car," I told Hardy before nodding to her and heading out.

"Car?" I heard her say.

I smiled on the way out the door.

Hardy left his car door unlocked. I shut the door behind me and called Trudy while I waited.

"Dakota! Are you okay?" she answered on the first ring. "We saw someone scream past the store, throw something in, and the next thing I knew there were cops and ambulances everywhere!"

"Someone broke into my house."

Trudy gasped. "What?"

"It was the same person who killed Tara."

"How do you know?"

"They left a note for me telling me to stay out of the case."

"You aren't involved!"

"I suspect they thought it was just a matter of time."

"That's strange," Trudy remarked. "Do you think they're from here?"

"Hardy thinks so."

She hummed. "I saw him with you," Trudy said casually.

"He asked me to move in with him."

Trudy inhaled and choked. I held the phone away from my ear.

"Come by as soon as you can. Tell me everything." She sounded giddy. "I'm at the store and have to run. Talk soon."

I grinned at the phone and tucked it back into my purse. Hardy walked out of the house, extricating Short from his arm. I watched him glance at her warily before he jogged down the steps.

"She seems nice," I said when we pulled away from the curb.

He jerked and slid me a sideways glance. "Short is new to the force."

"And in need of friends, I'm sure."

His lips quirked in a smile. "Perhaps she is. You should give her a call."

A surprised laugh broke from me. "Maybe I will," I said.

HARDY LIVED in a charming white house with a gorgeous wrap around porch a few miles outside of town. The closest neighbor looked to be at least a quarter of a mile away.

"You have a lot of land," I observed.

"It's the only house I wanted," he said as he held open the door to the guest house. It sat several feet away from the main house behind a lap pool and a built-in hot tub. Roses were twined in a pergola attached to the front–pink, purple, and white, right at the end of winter's bloom. Numerous other roses had tight buds waiting on the first blush of spring.

I stepped in and gaped. Burnished wood floors gleamed with high polish. The walls were painted a soft dove gray and the crown molding a bright creamy white. Cream colored couches surrounded a cheery fireplace, and above the flickering flame was a small LCD television set.

The kitchen was off to the right, full of brand-new stainless-steel appliances. White cabinets and a robin's egg blue island complimented the gray paint. "This is stunning," I managed when I could finally speak.

Relief flickered in his eyes. "The bedroom is this way." He led me through the small cottage. "There's a small seating area there with a computer desk if you need it. A half bath to the right, and the master is just up ahead. There's a full bath included."

I stopped at the entrance. "Are you sure? You could rent this place out for a mint."

"I don't want anyone else living on my property."

He took my bag and set it on the floor beside the bed. "I've made sure it's stocked with towels and washcloths and all the toiletries. If you need something else, let me know and I'll get it." Hardy tapped his fingers against his thighs. He looked...nervous.

"If I need any toiletries, I'll get them, but thank you."

"I'm serious. I can get them."

"Hardy." I touched his upper arm. "This is wonderful, and I can't thank you enough for allowing me to stay here. I plan on calling my insurance company in just a minute. The second I can move back in; I'll be out of here."

"You don't have to hurry."

My heart thumped. "I won't intrude for a moment longer."

"It's yours for as long as you need it." He put a key on the dresser, thumped the door jam, and left me alone.

Here I was. In Hardy's cottage. On his property.

So. Weird.

TEN

I slipped out early the next morning, the book Harriet had given me tucked in my purse. Trudy and I planned to meet at 6:30 to chat about Tara, though I knew I wouldn't escape chatting about Hardy. Speaking of, he'd pulled some strings so she could get back into her shop. She couldn't open yet, but at least she could bring in cleaners and prepare the shop for when the police allowed her to get back to business.

I tried not to look at my shop when I pulled up, but my gaze drifted over. Even though it was still dark, the damage couldn't be missed. The company Hardy called earlier had boarded up the window. It would be a while before I could have the bookstore decal replaced, but at least the glass would be repaired later today. Squaring my shoulders, I walked past and headed into Trudy's shop.

The smell of bleach assaulted my nose and I stopped in

my tracks. "Trudy?" I held my hand over my nose and mouth and ventured further into the store.

"Back here! Sorry about the smell. We might have to chat on the back patio."

"You have a back patio?" I asked as I headed back to the kitchen.

"Sure do." Trudy led me past the kitchen and outside, into a small area with a wooden deck and two iron tables. "Sit right here, honey, and I'll get you a coffee."

"Thanks, Trudy."

"Don't thank me yet. We have lots to talk about." With a wink, she headed back inside.

I tucked my jacket closer around me and dug my wool beanie out of my purse. The weather was still frigid, especially in the morning time. Coffee would warm me up and wake me up since I didn't see a coffee pot inside of the kitchen. I'd have to stop at the store to get one on my way back.

Trudy came out a few minutes later with a tray filled with coffee and goodies. She set it in front of me and doled out a chocolate chip scone and a croissant. "I didn't know which one you wanted, so I brought both. I had to throw away most of the ingredients in the fridge area, but I keep a smaller one stocked in the back. Everything here is fresh. I made them this morning, but since I can't open, I'm going to have to give them away. So eat up."

I gratefully accepted a scone and smeared some of the fresh honey butter Trudy had brought out.

"Do you know of anyone who doesn't want you to succeed?"

Trudy froze in the act of sitting. "You don't waste time, do you? The sun hasn't even risen yet."

I chewed thoughtfully and shook my head. "I'm staying in Hardy's guesthouse. Time is of the essence."

Her eyes widened comically. "Rewind. You're doing what??"

"Long story," I said, waving my hands. "My house was ransacked and took some damage. The insurance is sending out an adjuster today to look at everything, but I won't be able to move back in for a few weeks, I think."

"You're living with Hardy?" Trudy said, ignoring everything else I'd just told her.

"No. His guesthouse."

"Same thing," Trudy teased.

"Definitely not the same thing. I don't want this getting around town."

She leaned forward, her eyes sparkling in the dim light. "I also heard about him carrying you through the hospital like a knight in shining armor."

"I don't want to talk about that." My tone came out shorter than I intended. "Sorry," I said, deflating. "This is a lot to process right now, and Hardy is acting really weird. Is there anyone you can think of who may not want you to franchise?"

Trudy sat back and sipped her coffee, her brow furrowed in thought. "Honestly, I can't really think of anyone. We have our fair share of disgruntled customers, but there hasn't been anyone who's seemed upset about this. I haven't decided to franchise the store yet, either."

"But you are opening two more?"

She nodded. "At least two. I need to hire some more people, but after this I don't know if anyone will come work for me."

"What about family?"

Trudy blinked. "My sister wouldn't harm a fly and my brother has more money than Midas. Neither of them would do anything like this."

"Step siblings? Nieces, nephews?"

Trudy slowly shook her head. "My stepsister and I are pretty close. My nephew is a pretty good kid. He's in his late twenties now." Her gaze narrowed.

"What about this aunt? Who is she?"

"It's probably nothing." She tapped her fingers on the table.

"Every little detail matters." I wiggled my fingers. "Tell me."

"You know Connie?"

I'd seen her pop into *Sprinkle Heaven* a few times. "She's the red-haired woman with the green eyes? The one with the yellow Volvo?"

"That's the one. We aren't related. Her hair is Clairol." Trudy rolled her eyes. "She married my uncle after his first wife died. I've never seen a woman's eyes gleam like Connie's did when my uncle came into his inheritance."

I held up a finger. "Hold that thought." Rummaging through my purse, I pulled out an ink pen and a small notepad. "Okay. Go."

Trudy smirked at me. "Connie went nuts. They bought a pool and remodeled that old eighties wallpapered home. Then they bought the land next to it and expanded that too." She sighed. "My uncle was beside himself. The last time I saw him he was twenty pounds and about fifty grand lighter."

I asked the obvious question. "Is your uncle still alive?"

"He passed away about six months ago. Connie wore a designer suit and catered the most expensive Italian restaurant for the wake."

"Has she ever shown interest in your shop?"

Trudy tore off a piece of croissant and popped it in her mouth. "Only my cake," she quipped.

"Anyone else?"

"I'd rather talk about Hardy," she groaned.

"I'd rather get your shop reopened so you can ply me with lattes and baked goods." I scratched another note on the paper then looked up at her. "And I'm sure you'd like to continue getting a steady paycheck."

"Ah yes," Trudy said lightly. "Bills do need to be paid." She rubbed her eyes and sat up straight. "Okay. Let me think."

I sipped my coffee and scratched notes as she rattled off all the people she thought might have reason to want to sabotage her. Some I erased right away. Others I made notes next to. Most of them probably had nothing to do with it, but better safe than sorry.

"How long before you can open back up?"

She grimaced. "They think a week, maybe two."

"So you're saying I should hoard the rest of this scone?"

"Not at all. I made up two dozen and froze the dough for half of those."

"You are a queen among women," I said on a sigh.

"If I think of anything else, I'll drop by or send you a text." Trudy stood. "I have a lot to do to reopen but you can stay out here as long as you want."

"I'm a little jealous you didn't tell me about this back paradise before now."

"That's because I hardly ever get to enjoy it. But with the store closed, I have more time on my hands." Sadness settled into the lines of her face. "I hate to even ask you this…"

I held up my notepad. "I'm working on it."

She smiled sadly. "I hope we find out who did this soon. I have someone interested in opening a third store." Trudy opened the door and was about to step in.

"Wait!"

She stopped. "What?"

"You didn't mention you were opening a third store!"

"I didn't think it was pertinent."

"Of course it is. Everything is pertinent right now." I waved my notepad at her. "Tell me everything. Every little thing matters."

Trudy tapped her temple. "I'll remember that. Pop inside if you want another cup of coffee."

"I'll definitely do that."

"Thanks, Dakota."

I waved her away and settled in to try to make sense of what my notes said.

ELEVEN

I'd just drained the rest of my coffee when a rustling from the bush several feet over caught my attention. The back of the shops was mostly abandoned. There were a few parking areas, but most of it backed up to greenery. The last time I'd been out back I'd had a run in with a killer, but I hadn't noticed Trudy's seating area. If I had, I would have been out here much more often. There were enough cars around to keep a lot of the wildlife away, but we still had a lot of squirrels and the occasional racoon. I assumed it was one of those, but I overheard what sounded suspiciously like whispers. Careful to keep from clinking my mug against Trudy's saucer, I stood and crept over to the side of the building to listen.

"Is she there?" a man whispered.

"I saw someone go in. Had to be Trudy."

I pulled out my cell phone and texted Hardy. Harder than I expected it to be with only one hand.

Behind Trudy's shop. Two people hiding in the bush.

Three little dots appeared almost immediately. *Get out of there. I'll call it in.*

Don't call it in! I'm listening!

Dakota. No.

Give me five minutes.

He didn't respond, but I had no doubt he was already peeling rubber out of his driveway.

"Do you think she has it?"

I crept closer. *Has what?*

"It wasn't in the shop the first time I checked."

"It has to be somewhere."

I took a step closer. Wood underneath my feet creaked. I winced and waited.

"The sun is coming up. We need to get out of here."

"We can't leave until we have it!"

"We'll have another opportunity. The shop isn't open yet."

I stayed quiet and still as a mouse in danger.

The door behind me opened. "Dakota? I brought you another coffee. It's chilly out and I thought you might want another."

A muffled curse came from the bush. I jumped off the deck, wincing as my arm jarred against my side. "Hey!"

Two figures burst from the brush, the first a tall, skinny man and the second a shorter, slender woman. At least I thought it was a woman. Both were dressed in black, their hair concealed underneath black beanie caps. They ran past me in a blur. I chased after them, but I didn't have a body built for speed. I had a body built for coffee, scones, and reading. Within seconds, they'd outran me, disappearing into the back woods behind the shops.

"What on Earth!" Trudy called. She stopped beside me and bent over with her hands on her knees, huffing and puffing.

Hardy skidded around the corner; gun drawn. He wore his cop face, blank and intense. "Where?"

I pointed in the direction of the woods. Without a word, Hardy ran into the depths, his weapon down at his side.

Trudy sighed next to me. "If you don't take him, I will."

Hardy disappeared into the dense cover, and I think he might have taken a piece of my heart with him. Trudy put a hand on my arm. "Don't."

I realized I had taken several steps forward.

"He'll be fine. He's trained for this."

"This is Silverwood. No one is trained for this." My heart pounded in my chest as I waited for Hardy to return. A few moments later, the sound of sirens rounded the bend and soon enough, three other police officers rushed past us and into the woods behind Hardy.

"They were asking about you," I said into the silence.

"Me?"

"They were talking about whether you had *it*." I glanced at her. "What is *it*?"

Trudy looked away, but not before I caught a flash of what looked like fear.

"Trudy?"

"I have no idea." Her hand fluttered to her throat. "I don't have anything except a whole lot of debt from the shop." Trudy's smile wobbled. She wrung her hands and wiped them on her apron. "I should offer them coffee," she said and spun on her heel.

I watched her walk away, wondering what she was hiding from me.

LESS THAN FIVE MINUTES LATER, Hardy walked out of the woods. He'd holstered his weapon and strode toward me. I swallowed hard watching his approach. He had a leaf in his hair, and I longed to brush it away.

Oh boy. I was in *deep* trouble.

"Did you find them?" I blurted before he could say anything. Despite evidence to the contrary, I couldn't help but fill the silence before I said something dumb.

"They're still looking." He stopped a foot away. "Are you okay?"

"I'm fine. I overheard them sneaking around, but Trudy came out before I could overhear much."

His face shuttered and Hardy ran a hand through his hair. "This is difficult, Dakota."

I steeled my spine and waited. If he said one thing, I would turn around and walk away from him, and I would drive straight to that cottage and pack my things.

Silence stretched. Birds sang in the trees as the sun slowly made its way over the horizon. The police radios crackled and beeped, though there wasn't much traffic on them right now. Gentle wind blew through the trees, sending the leaves on the ground rustling. It was the beginning of a beautiful day, and I wondered whether it would stay that way.

He tilted his face up to the sky, squinted, and took two steps toward me. Moments later, he gathered me in his arms, carefully avoiding my broken arm, and swept his lips over mine.

Whoa.

He rested his forehead against mine and we stood that way, his arms around my waist and one of mine around his neck. "Just be careful," he said after a moment.

A loud wolf whistle rang out. Hardy and I jerked apart. I wiped my free hand down my thigh and laughed nervously. "Well."

Short interrupted by stepping in between us. Her gaze lingered on me before she turned to Hardy. "We lost them. There's a trail leading out to another parking lot a mile or so back. We think they may have parked their car there."

"Surveillance cameras?"

"They're checking." Short didn't acknowledge my presence. She turned so her profile was to me, her posture stiff and tense.

"Good. Let me know what you find." Hardy dismissed her, but Short lingered until his eyebrows went up. "Anything else?"

Short's gaze flicked to me.

I pulled my phone out and turned away. Whatever she wanted to say to him, she didn't want me to hear. Trudging back up Trudy's steps, I checked my texts. Daniel had sent me one about five minutes ago.

Looking for you. Trudy said you were at the back of her shop. I have coffee.

I tensed.

The second one was sent a minute later.

You look busy. Perhaps we should talk.

I touched my lips with my fingertips before going inside and cutting through Trudy's shop.

When had life become so complicated?

TWELVE

A few minutes later I was back in my shop. Poppy had decided to stay in Hardy's cottage, content to check all the new things out. Hopefully she stayed away from his furniture. The shop was quiet and clean, and it was still early enough for the tourists to still be tucked in their beds. I still had a couple of hours before I opened, so I headed to the office to try to figure out what to say to Daniel.

I had a lot of decisions to make. Hardy represented an unexpected kink in my plans. I'd written him off and perhaps that was a mistake. He might not like the way I did things, but he hadn't lost interest in me. Daniel was an interesting, intelligent man who shared many of the same hobbies with me. Sighing, I rubbed my eyes and tossed my cell onto the desk.

I wasn't ready to make any decisions, and this wasn't something that should be a priority. My house lay in shambles and my friend's restaurant was shut down. The two were connected and if I didn't find out who'd done it, my shop might be next.

My cell pinged. I picked it up and saw a text message from the company Hardy hired to fix my broken shop window. There was an opening due to a cancellation and they wanted to know if I was available now.

I texted back and invited them to come over. If they could get it fixed today, I could open with no issues. If I tried to open with the window the way it was, most people would pass my place right on by.

They'd be here in twenty minutes. In the meantime, I pulled my notes back out and tried to connect some dots.

Trudy had something they wanted. Who *they* was happened to be beyond me right now, but it was for sure a man and a woman.

Maybe Connie.

I frowned as I looked down at her name and texted Trudy.

Can Connie bake?

If it comes in a box and has two ingredients.

Her snarky reply made me laugh. Why would a woman who couldn't bake want to sabotage Trudy? It's not like Trudy would leave her the store. Would she?

Do you have your estate planning complete?

The pause in her response was longer. *I do.* The three dots kept starting and stopping periodically. *Why?*

Connie isn't in it, is she?

Not a chance. Relieved, I was about to cross her name off, but her next response stayed my hand. *But my niece is.*

Do they know?

They shouldn't, she responded, *but I've spoken with Demi about the shop before.*

Is she interested?

She loves to bake and she loves to come here and watch me work. I have to say yes.

She couldn't be cleared yet. *How old is your niece?*

Twenty-one.

Definitely not. *Thanks, Trudy. I'll let you know what else I find out. Keep me posted about what the police say. If you think of anything else, let me know.*

You don't think my niece has anything to do with this?

Nothing is off the table.

I added Demi to my notes. Then I started a separate category for competing businesses. We didn't have any that could compete with Trudy's wizardry in the kitchen. Maybe that was the issue. I tapped the pencil against my cheek. Was there a way to find out about any pending business licenses? That might be a good way to find out who was opening what and if Trudy's plans would make it more difficult for them. There was only one place for rent downtown right now and it happened to be right next to *Sprinkle Heaven.*

A knock on the door made me put my pencil down, but I picked up my purse and phone. I wanted to pay Jen over at *Olive Twist!* a visit to see if she'd seen anything. We weren't as good of friends as Trudy and I were, but we still got along well. Jen was a good business neighbor, though she kept to herself much more than most of the people around here did.

The man standing outside was an older gentleman with an iron-colored handlebar mustache and steel gray hair. He wore a clean uniform with the name Stan's Glassworks embroidered on the pocket of his slate blue button down.

"Ms. Adair?" he said, reading from his clipboard.

"That's me."

"I'm Stan Holder. Hardy Cavanaugh hired me to repair your glass." He grimaced at the wood nailed up. "Please accept my apologies for not getting to it last night."

"Not at all," I said, waving his apologies away. "I'm grateful you're here now."

"I have a photo of the previous window. Do you happen to have the logo in PNG format? It would be easier for me to recreate it if you do."

Hope flared within me. "Your company can do that?"

He looked at me over the small wire-framed glasses perched on his nose. "We can and we do. We specialize in regular and stained glass, glass etching, and logos installation on said glass."

"I'll dig it out for you. This is wonderful news."

Stan gave me a polite smile and handed over his business card. "That's a good email address. Send it there and I'll try to have it turned around in 24 hours."

"Amazing," I murmured. "I have an errand to run right next door, but when it's finished, I'll dig it out of my computer files and get it sent to you." Holding open the door, I motioned for Stan to come in. "There's coffee and tea on the small table there. Make yourself at home." I peered out at the road. "Are you by yourself?"

"For now. My son will be joining me in about an hour."

"Oh good. I'll leave you to it, then."

Stan nodded. "We'll be out of your hair by tonight. The logo should go up first thing in the morning if you're here."

"Tell me what time and I'll make sure I'm here."

He squinted. "I figure about 8."

"Then I'll be here by 7:30."

Stan nodded and I left him there staring at the window as if it were speaking to him. Maybe it did. I wasn't all that into window repair.

MAYBE JEN and I weren't better friends because I couldn't handle having two talented bakers in my repertoire. Trudy had put a good five pounds on me over the last couple of months, so I avoided going into Jen's shop just in case she did the same. Now, walking in and smelling the buttery garlic scent always lingering in the shop made me regret that decision.

"Dakota?" Jen popped her head up from the display case.

"Hey Jen. You have a second to talk?"

"Of course." She held up a pair of tongs and clacked them together as one always does when holding a set. "I have a new black garlic and brioche if you want to try it."

Heaven help me. "Does anyone ever tell you no when you ask questions like that?"

She grinned and ducked back into the case. "Only if they have gluten intolerance. And isn't that a terrible fate?"

Jen was a pretty, slim and fit forty-something. She leaned toward athletic gear and a high ponytail even when she was working in her shop. The place was warm and homey and lined from floor to ceiling with all of her oil and vinegar concoctions, many of which I'd already tried and loved.

Jen came out from behind the counter with a few slices of the bread with a small container of what looked to be an herby dip. "Olive oil, garlic, rosemary, and red pepper," she said as she held it out.

"This smells like heaven." I took the plate and let her lead me over to the back. She slid in the booth opposite me.

"Is this about Trudy?"

I paused in the middle of my bite, and she laughed. Setting the bread down, I dug into my purse and retrieved my notepad and pencil.

"You hardly ever come by, and I'd have to be blind not to notice all the police over her shop. Plus, you know how this town is." Jen rolled her eyes.

"Have you seen anyone at her shop that looks like they don't belong?"

Both of her eyebrows rose. "There are tourists here every single day. I don't know who belongs and who doesn't."

"Anyone suspicious? Have you overheard anything about Trudy's new stores?"

Jen's eyes flashed at that. "Everyone's heard about Trudy's expansion. I don't know that a lot of people are happy about it."

I lifted my head from my notes. "Oh?"

A look of regret crossed her face. "Look, you didn't hear this from me, but there's a lot of people in town who don't want Silverwood to grow and expand. They like it just the way it is."

"Trudy's shops are all out of town. I don't see why it would bother them."

Jen tilted her head. "You haven't heard."

"I'm not sure what you mean."

Jen snorted. "Dakota, I swear. You're like an ostrich sometimes."

A little stung, I bristled and set my pencil down. "If there's something I'm missing, I'd love to be caught up to speed."

"Trudy is in a bidding war for the property next door."

My heart skipped a beat. "Excuse me?

She nodded. "She and a few other people have been duking it out for three weeks now."

I sat back and chewed thoughtfully. "Do you know who's bidding against her?"

Jen shrugged. "No idea. The only reason I know it's Trudy is because her niece said something about it when she came in here looking for a job."

"Demi wants to work here?"

Jen laughed. "She's young. She doesn't want to work anywhere. I guess her aunt is making her get a job."

Interesting. "I thought the property was for lease, not for sale."

"With enough money, anything can be bought."

Her tone was light, but there was a sharp note in it. I tucked my pen and notebook away. "And how are you?"

Jen sighed. "I'm fine. Things are a little weird right now with all the crime, but business is good."

I chewed on another piece of bread. "What do you think about Trudy?" I asked after a bit.

"Her expansion?"

I nodded.

Jen shrugged and scratched her chin. "It happens everywhere. At least she's not a corporate chain. I think that would make it worse for me. She's a small store with home baked goods. We could do worse."

The words were sincere, but her tone was off. "How long have you lived here?"

Her brow furrowed at the question. "My entire life. I love this place."

"Me too," I said as I looked out the window. "Trudy's is shut down for now. Hopefully a week or two at most. Do you know when the auction will be over?"

Jen shook her head. "No idea. It's online, I think. Everyone knows Trudy's handle, but the other two are mysteries."

I pulled out a ten and put it on the table.

"It's not necessary–" she began.

"The new bread is wonderful," I interrupted. "You should definitely carry it."

Jen didn't argue anymore, but I felt her eyes on me all the way out.

UNSETTLED, I decided not to open the shop. Stan and his son were hard at work with the new glass panel, so I popped back inside and went back to my notes. The meeting with Jen unsettled me and I wasn't sure why. She was right on several points. Silverwood was a small town. Few people here liked change. The town skewed older and many of the older residents resented when a business expanded or something new opened. Unless, of course, they were the ones opening it. We had children, of course, but the vast majority of the population was thirty or above. I was one of the minority, even though I was getting up there.

Jen had a nice sized shop right in the middle of the tourist area, just like I did. Trudy, as well. It seemed like the most obvious thing for Trudy was buying the property next to hers, knocking down some walls and expanding. Though I did think it was weird she didn't tell me. That seemed like the kind of thing you'd tell a good friend.

Unless maybe she didn't think of me as a good friend? The thought of that sent a rock in my belly and made me feel uncomfortable about broaching the subject. If someone was outbidding her on the building, who was it, and why did they care so much? Disturbed, I picked up the phone and called Cole.

"You need something, don't you?" he said without bothering to say hello. "Is this about Trudy?"

"Hi Cole. Perhaps I was calling to ask you to lunch."

I could almost hear his eyes roll. "Okay, first of all, no one except you says *perhaps* and you only say it when you're trying to be prissy."

That startled a laugh out of me. "Prissy?" I asked in mock outrage.

"Yes, *prissy*. It's the voice you always get when I ask if you're looking into something and you pretend you're not and get all bothered by my assumptions."

I gave up the pretense. "Fine. Can you look into something for me?"

"Depends on what it is and if it can get me in trouble. If it can get me into trouble, my answer is a resounding yes, because it's been ages since you've involved me in your shenanigans."

I snorted. "I'm afraid there are few shenanigans. I'm trying to figure out if there's a way to search for pending business licenses."

I could hear Cole tapping something on his desk. "Hmm. There is. It depends on whether they've masked their identity, though."

"Someone can do that?"

"Oh yes, my friend. People can shield under layers and layers of shell companies. Granted, usually only massive corporations or billionaires do that, but weirder things have happened in this strange little town of ours."

"Is there a way to find out who's bidding on a property?"

"Ah." Cole chuckled. "I see you've stumbled on the same tidbit we have. You're talking about the property right next door to Trudy, aren't you?"

"Yes." I sighed heavily. "Let me guess. You can't figure it out?"

"I've tried. Whoever is doing it is using a VPN. I'm not too savvy with computers, so it's beyond me. We have our IT department working on it, but so far, no dice."

"Bummer." I thought for a second. "What is a VPN exactly?"

"I'm not exactly sure. It's something you use when you want to hide your IP address or when you want to search another country's internet."

"Like if I wanted to watch the UK version of Netflix?"

"Specific example, but yet," Cole said with a chuckle. "People use it when they're traveling so they can continue to access their bank accounts and what not. People here use it for browsing privacy. It's not uncommon, but they use them a lot for unsavory things too."

I thought about that for a moment. "I don't understand why someone would use it for something like that."

"Maybe Trudy would know who they are?" He didn't sound sure about that.

"Would it matter?"

"Maybe there's history between them. Maybe she has a competitor who's trying to undercut her."

"All this over a restaurant?" I wondered aloud.

"You'd be surprised at the lengths people would go to when they want to see someone fail." Another voice came over the line, muffled and indistinct. It sounded like Cole covered the mouthpiece for a second before he came back on the line. "I have to go. I'll find out what I can and let you know, but we're already on this and so far haven't uncovered anything. Whoever is doing it is covering their tracks."

"Thanks, Cole."

"You bet. Talk soon?"

"Of course." We hung up and I put my head down on the desk. I was still trying not to think about Trudy's withholding of information that could help her. Not telling me meant she had something to hide. If she had something to hide, could she be withholding other information? Like about Tara?

The thought sent a chill through me. I couldn't believe that of my friend because if Trudy was capable of something like that, then I couldn't trust anyone.

A knock on the office door jerked me out of my maudlin thoughts.

"Ms. Adair?" Stan stood right outside. "We have the window placed and sealed. Make sure you don't touch it tonight or for the first few hours tomorrow. Once you come in and open, it should be good to go. I think we'll come a little later to replace your decal, but I expect tomorrow we'll be out of your hair for good."

I gave him a tired smile. "Thank you, Stan. How much do I owe you?" I rummaged through the desk for my checkbook, but he shook his head. "No. It's all covered."

"By Hardy?" The thought of it made color creep up my face.

"Not quite. The Silverwood Police Department." Stan smiled. "Damage like this happens more often than you think."

"Well, I guess that's both frightening and comforting." I stood from behind the desk and walked over to shake his hand. "I appreciate you getting me in so quickly."

"It's our pleasure, ma'am. We'll see you first thing in the morning."

I walked Stan out, surprised to see the sun had already fallen below the horizon. I'd been so tied up with putting puzzle pieces together I'd completely lost track of time. Juggling my keys, I unlocked the door for the workers and stepped outside for a breath of fresh air only to see Hardy leaning on my car.

"Hi."

He was so handsome he took my breath away. Dark hair, blue eyes, the smile crinkling the edges of them. "Hi," I repeated dumbly.

"I wanted to make sure you were okay. You didn't open the shop today."

I jerked a thumb toward the window. "They were working on the window all day and thought I might lose business if I opened so I just took the day for myself."

"Want me to follow you home?"

Home. I blinked and Hardy blushed as he realized what he said.

"Err. The cottage is what I meant."

"I have something else to take care of but thank you." We stood there staring at each other for a moment. "Could you pop in and make sure Poppy hasn't destroyed the furniture?"

A look of alarm crossed his face before he realized I was somewhat joking. "Ah. Of course. Want me to save you some dinner?"

I shook my head, dreading what I had to do. "I'm not hungry right now, but I'll grab something later."

"Alright then," he said and pushed away from my car. "Call if you need anything."

I smiled and waved. "I will."

Hardy walked a few spots over, got in his car, and turned toward his home. I watched him for a few moments before I sighed and headed back inside. What I had to do would not be easy.

THIRTEEN

The phone rang twice.

"Dakota."

"Hi Daniel."

"I still want us to be friends," he said before I could say anything else.

I blinked and lost my train of thought.

"We aren't committed to each other. We've never been on a date. I like you, Dakota, even if it never goes any further."

Tears filled my eyes. "I'd like that," I choked out. "I don't know what's happening between Hardy and me, but I feel like I need to see where it goes."

"You have history."

I laughed. "Not a lot, but some. It got really weird between us..." I trailed off. "You don't want to hear this."

Daniel sighed over the line. "I want you to be happy. That's all. You're the first person I've met who had no idea who I was and who wanted to be friends with me because of *me*. That doesn't come around too often."

"You're one in a million, Daniel. I'd like to stay friends for as long as we can, but I can't promise anything further right now."

"I wouldn't expect you to."

"Good."

"How's Trudy's case going?"

I groaned and told him some of the things I'd found out. When I got to the part of the VPN, Daniel interrupted.

"I might be able to help. Potentially."

Excitement welled up in me. "Truly?"

"Don't get too excited yet. I had to do some research on VPNs for my last book. I believe if you interrupt the service, you might be able to uncover the IP address and identity of the person using it."

"The VPN service?" That seemed difficult.

"Yes. It's easier said than done, but I had a...friend. He's experienced with these kinds of things."

"Like a hacker?"

"Err. Something like that. If you give me the pertinent details, I can pass them on and see if he can help."

"There's an auction site for a building Trudy is interested in buying, but someone keeps outbidding her. No one can tell who it is, though Trudy isn't masking her identity. Is there any way to tell who the other bidder is? If we can, we might be able to pinpoint the murderer."

"You think it's someone trying to compete with her?"

I stood and stretched my back. The delicious stretch made me groan. I'd sat for too long today. "I'm not entirely sure. There aren't a lot of people here who'd be interested in bidding on something like that. Cole is looking into new business licenses to see if anyone is planning on opening up a competing business, but he's having a difficult time with the VPN."

"Let me worry about it," Daniel said. "Besides, this will help the second book in the series."

"I appreciate this so much. What can I do for you?"

"You can show up next week with a lemon cake and a bottle of that good white blend you brought over last month. I have the chess board. Game?"

Relief speared through me. "You're on. But don't cry when you lose again."

Daniel's warm chuckle rolled over the line. "You might get lucky once, but skill always overrules luck."

"We'll see." We said our goodbyes and hung up. As soon as the line went dead, I inhaled a shaky breath. I liked Daniel. A lot. I liked Hardy too. They were wildly different. Hardy had a protective, authoritative streak. Daniel was intellectual and soft spoken, and he appealed to my literary heart. Hardy struggled with who I was, but he seemed to care about me anyway. I thought that showed a strength of heart and a desire to go for what he wanted despite all the ways it could go wrong.

I didn't know Daniel well enough to know much else about him, though I did know I enjoyed spending time with him.

Either way, I wasn't ready to commit to anyone right now. There were still too many issues to work out. But I wouldn't object to a few more stolen kisses from Hardy. With a groan, I locked Tattered Pages up and headed back to the cottage.

POPPY LAY CURLED up on the sofa, barely raising her head to look at me when I walked in. She gave me a pitiful yowl and promptly shut her eyes. Grinning despite myself, I filled her bowl with food and made sure she still had water before I slipped away to change. When I came back to the kitchen, I opened the fridge and saw a bowl with a note attached to it. Curious, I pulled it toward me.

I made this last night and thought you might like it. It's Zuppa Toscana, one of my favorites.

With a shrug, I tugged the lid off and poured some into a ceramic bowl to reheat. There was a new loaf of crusty bread right by the stove, so I cut myself a couple of slices of it and slathered it generously with butter. When the microwave dinged, I gathered everything up and headed over to the table to eat. If I were in my own house, I would have sprawled on the couch with my food and drinks, but this wasn't mine and I'd be mortified if I spilled anything on Hardy's couch.

What a day. As things went, it wasn't as productive as I would have liked, but I did have feelers out about Trudy. I only hoped she would come out unscathed in this whole mess.

I blew on the soup and took a bite. There were hints of basil, oregano, fennel, and red pepper. I stirred my spoon through the bowl and investigated. Italian sausage. Potatoes. Kale. Onions and some kind of broth. The soup was delicious and went well with the bread and wine I'd chosen. Hardy had left four bottles–two white and two red. I'd opened the white one–a somewhat dry Pinot Grigio with a fruity finish.

The kitchen table was right next to the back window. He'd left the curtains open, and moonlight spilled into the backyard. I couldn't make out all of the plants, but there were a few plants with small white flowers blooming and a lot of bright chartreuse greenery. This place was comfy and cozy, and I was surprised to find myself comfortable here. I set my laptop on the table and turned it on. My email had been dinging like crazy today, and I'd been so distracted I failed to check it. Harper would be back in a couple of days so I needed to get some things done in the store so she wouldn't come back to complete chaos.

Tomorrow would be a busy day. The adjuster had rescheduled for the afternoon via voicemail. I'd missed the call this morning with all the action and hadn't thought to check it until I was on the way home tonight. Hopefully everything would be covered by the policy, but if it wasn't, I didn't lose anything overly sentimental. Everything was replaceable, though if someone had damaged more than the window in my shop, I'm not sure I'd be as optimistic about everything. There were too many valuable books in

Tattered Pages. If I lost any of them, I would be devastated.

Poppy stretched and bounded across the room to bump me with her head. I scratched her behind her ear three times before I turned my attention back to my soup. She was a typical cat. If Poppy allowed you to touch her, you could only pet her so many times before she'd hiss and try to nail you with her claws. I'd grown wise to her wily ways less than two weeks after I'd gotten her, even if Poppy tried to trick me by bumping me again and meowing pitifully.

"I'll pet you as long as you want, but I won't let you bite me, you little savage," I said affectionately. Poppy whipped her tail up and turned, showing me her rear end as she sashayed over to her food.

My email dinged as soon as I opened it up. Dozens of unread emails stared back at me accusingly. With a sigh, I clicked on the first and began to read.

TWENTY MINUTES LATER, just as my eyes started to droop, I hovered the mouse over a name that felt somewhat familiar. Realization struck me in an instant and I jerked upright, sending Poppy yowling off the table in fright.

"Sorry, sorry," I cajoled.

Poppy glared at me and re-took her original position on the sofa.

Jeff's agent had emailed me back. I opened the email, skimmed quickly, and jumped out of my chair fist-pumping. She'd even given me his direct email address.

"Score!" I whisper yelled.

I got up to make a cup of coffee before I emailed him back. It was only nine p.m., but I was already wiped out. I'd send this email, hit the sack, and try to get to the store as early as possible. I needed Jeff to come out as soon as possible, so if he was agreeing, I had a lot of marketing to do to make sure we had a good crowd.

THE NEXT MORNING, I made it to Tattered Pages with a grumpy cat in tow and an extra-large tumbler of coffee. Stan and his son sat in front of the shop waiting for me.

"You're early!" I exclaimed as I hurried to unlock the door.

"A little," Stan said. "We have a busy workday ahead of us and wanted to get as early of a start as possible."

I flipped on the lights and motioned them in. "I'll start some coffee."

His son was maybe my age. A little on the shorter side, but lean and well dressed. Probably too well-dressed for the job he had. I hurried over to the coffee pot while they set themselves up and when it was finished dripping, I brought them both to go mugs filled to the brim. Those would keep it warmer for longer while they worked.

"Thanks," the son said gratefully. Stan just grunted.

"Do you like working for your dad?" I asked. Stan was busy measuring the window and had already tuned the world out.

His son blinked. "I don't work for him," he said with

surprise. "I just help him out when he needs it. There's been a shortage of glassworkers in town for a while now and Dad is overwhelmed with all the work."

"Oh! I'm so sorry. I just assumed."

He pushed his glasses up. "I work in tech, specifically in cybersecurity."

My interest piqued as I thought about my current predicament. "If you have time when you get off, do you mind chatting with me about something?"

"Reese, by the way," he said and held out his hand. "I think we'll be finished by ten. Dad's in a hurry, but if you don't mind dropping me down the road so he can take the truck, I'd be happy to chat."

"No problem. I can shut down for a little while if need be."

"Great." Reese held the cup of coffee up and went over to help his dad while I headed to the back.

An email from Jeff awaited me.

He agreed to a signing four days from now.

No pressure.

FOURTEEN

A knock on the door came a few hours later. Knee deep in planning out spring's new inventory, I jerked at the sound. Reese stood at the door, an apology written on his face.

I let out a startled laugh. "Sorry. Ordering new inventory gets intense around here."

He smiled. "We just finished up if you want to take a look. Dad agreed to take the truck, so I'm going to need a ride if you're still offering."

"Absolutely." I pushed away from the desk and followed him out. My breath caught in my throat as I looked at the logo. "That's..."

Stan winced. "It was Hardy's idea. He thought you would like it."

Well, it was presumptive and annoying and...amazing. It was still my logo but bumped up by a thousand. The typography was bolder and better and slightly larger. He'd situated it so that it sat partially on top of a stack of books, but the best part about it was the cat curled up on top.

He'd made a likeness of Poppy. Tears sprang to my eyes and threatened to spill.

"I told him if you didn't like it that I'd scrape it right off and charge him twice," Stan groused.

I held up a hand. "No. It's...wonderful. I love it." And I did. The new logo was beautiful. What I didn't like was Hardy's assumption, though. I'd talk to him about it, but there was nothing I'd change about the way it looked. "You've done a stunning job."

Stan looked away, but I saw a hint of color creep up his cheeks. "Thank you, Ms. Adair. Reese here says you wanted to chat about some computer whatnot?"

"I do. I'd be happy to drop him off at your next job site."

Stan grunted. "It's close enough to walk, but if you've offered, I'm sure he'd be happy to take you up on it."

"Dad." Reese rolled his eyes. "It's three miles down the road."

"When I was your age..."

"Please don't," Reese groaned, but it was with affection and not annoyance. "Everyone knows how many miles you walked through the snow."

Stan's eyes twinkled as he gathered up his tools. "You got an hour. If you're any later than that, I'm going to tell your mother you're the cause of my current back pain."

Reese shook his head and watched him leave. "That old man is more than a pain in my back."

I laughed and motioned for him to sit. "I won't take up too much of your time. I'm interested in VPNs."

Reese's eyebrows rose. "They're pretty simple overall, but I'm surprised to hear you're thinking about using one."

"Oh no," I shook my head. "Not me. There's someone using one and we can't figure out who it is."

His eyes narrowed. "And why would you want to do that? They're private for a reason."

Sensing I was losing him, I started over. "Sorry. Let me explain." I breezed over the murder part of the story because something like that isn't how you get a stranger to trust you. When I got to the auction part, his head cleared.

"You think the person using the VPN is the same person who committed the crime." He scrubbed a hand over his chin. "I know who you are now."

I groaned and Reese laughed. "I should have put two and two together. You're the only bookstore owner in town." He reached into his bag and pulled out a computer. "What's the auction site?"

I sat closer to him and rattled the web address off. Reese pulled it up and searched for the auction. When he found it, I gasped in surprise. The property had gone way past a million. Way higher than what other properties went for around here. "This it?"

"It is."

"Only two bidders? Seems unusual."

"It's a small town. Most people rent around here." I hadn't wanted to rent when I got here. Tattered Pages would be mine for as long as I could hold onto it. The money sitting in my bank account came to mind again. When this was all over, I planned to go down to the bank and pay it off. After what happened to my house, I was no longer sure I wanted to stay there. Property values had gone up just in the short time since I'd bought it, so if I sold, I should be able to make a small profit on it.

Reese typed quickly, flipping back and forth between pages. "The property is owned by a company. I've never heard of the person in charge of it." I peered over his shoulder, but the name didn't mean anything to me either. Most of the buildings were stand-alone and owned by different people, so this wasn't surprising. "It looks like the first person, SprinkleHeaven, might be auto-bidding."

"What's that?"

"It's usually a program. They set a certain number they're willing to pay. When the cost goes above it, new bids are computer-generated. For example, if the other person went past 2.2 million and Trudy was willing to pay 2.3 million, the computer would automatically put in a new bid higher than the one the other person put in."

"What if it went past 2.3 million?"

Reese kept typing. "It would depend on how she set it up. If she didn't have a bid past 2.3 million and the auction ended with the other person's last bid, she would lose."

"Can she set it up to not bid right away?"

Reese shrugged. "It depends on the program she's using. Usually, yes, though."

I sat back and crossed my arm. "Huh." I didn't think

Trudy was that well off. Comfortable, yes. "Is this auction for cash?"

Reese didn't say anything for a minute as he skimmed the terms. He blew out a whistle. "Yes. The terms state the winner would pay cash and take immediate possession of the property."

Trudy had over two million in the bank? "What if the winner doesn't have it?"

"Then the next highest bid would be accepted, and the other bidder would win it."

"Do you think it's possible the second person might be driving the price higher on purpose?"

"Normally I would say yes, but this particular site requires a peek into the bank account of the bidder."

"Whoa," I said with feeling.

"Is this the bakery next door?" Reese asked.

I nodded. "It's a coffee shop and bakery. She's opening up a few more stores."

"Then it makes sense that she's trying to buy this property."

Yes, but she didn't say anything to me about it, I grumbled inside my head.

Reese tapped at the computer for a while, so I got up to get us both another coffee. Food would have to be added soon because I was getting a tad jittery. When I set the coffee down to the side of his computer, he glanced up with a weird look on his face.

"Everything okay?"

"You said SprinkleHeaven is bidding against someone, right?"

"I did. Why?"

Reese didn't say anything for a long moment. He picked up the coffee, took a sip, and stared at his computer before shaking his head.

When he told me the reason why he was asking, I sank to the couch, my heart feeling like it was being squeezed in a vise.

I had the reputation of being somewhat of a loner. Yes, I participated in festivals and the like, but I had yet to make relationships with most of the townspeople. I thought it might be awkward to approach people with weird small talk. I didn't care about things like the weather. I'd rather talk about deep and interesting topics and form a relationship that way. The problem was most people didn't do it that way. Looking back, I think Trudy and I became friends because of proximity. Jen and I circled around each other, but perhaps she had the same thought I did. Making friends as an adult seemed like a nightmare.

Reese sat beside me as I drove him down the road to the next job site. Once he'd figured out who was using the other VPN, conversation had all but died between us. After I thanked him profusely and offered to pay him, Reese had shut his computer and declined. I think the information rattled him some too because it spoke to something even more sinister than either of us would have imagined.

The entire thing had me sick to my stomach.

We passed out of downtown and toward the border of Silverwood. Candlelight Springs and most of the other places I frequented were the other way, so I rarely came out here.

"Right here," Reese said, pointing several feet ahead where there was a new structure being built. Around the freshly poured foundation sat several work trucks from different places around town. Six people struggled to unload a massive marquee sign that said *Connie's Coffee & Cookies*. I frowned at it and looked back at the new building. It didn't look like much right now, but when it was finished, I thought it might be twice the size of my bookstore. Rather large for a coffee shop.

A woman with faded red hair wearing ripped blue jeans came around the corner. My heart stopped.

Connie. Trudy's Connie.

My goodness. Now everything was coming together.

"The structure isn't even all the way up yet," I said. "Do you always do work this early?"

Reese pushed his glasses up. "I go where Dad tells me. It does seem pretty early, but he mentioned this woman wasn't easy to work for. Maybe he just needs me here for support."

I unbuckled my seatbelt. "I'll get out with you. I'd like to speak with the owner for a minute."

He gave me a curious look but shrugged and got out. "It was nice meeting you, Ms. Adair. I hope you get this all figured out." Reese looked around and lowered his voice.

"But please leave me out of this if you do. I'd rather not explain how I arrived at the conclusion I did."

I mimed zipping my lips shut. "Don't worry. We never spoke about this."

Relief filled his face. "Good luck. Dad is waving at me and doesn't look happy, so I need to go."

I waved and made my way over to Connie just as my cell rang. "Dakota," I said without looking at the caller ID.

"I just came across something you might want to know. Good idea on running the upcoming business licenses."

Connie looked up and frowned when she saw me. "Let me guess, Connie's Coffee and Cookies?"

Cole made a noise of disbelief. "I swear. How do you always find this stuff out before me?"

"Bad luck, I think," I said as I stopped in front of Trudy's aunt. "I have to go, but I'll call you back in just a few minutes."

"Can't wait. I want to hear all about it."

"Dakota Adair," Connie said.

"Ms. Connie," I acknowledged. "I had no idea you were opening up your own place."

She looked at her new shop with pride. "I've always wanted to. It seemed like a great time."

"How does Trudy feel about it?"

Her gaze sharpened. "Trudy and I aren't on speaking terms right now," she said in a clipped tone.

"Too bad. I heard she's expanding." The construction vehicles had spread out all over the place.

Connie's mouth turned down. "At the expense of our family," she muttered.

My interest sharpened. "Oh?"

She blew out a breath. "Nothing. Forget I even mentioned it."

"It's just that I noticed the shop next to Trudy's was for sale." I hedged a little. "I thought about tossing my hat in the ring for it, but I don't want to upset her."

Her eyes flashed with anger. "Trudy would fight you tooth and nail for it. Trust me. When it comes to business, she has no friends."

"That doesn't sound like the Trudy I know."

Connie laughed, a bitter sound. "Then she wants something from you."

I blinked. Did she want something from me? My stomach filled with acid. Our shops were right next door to each other...

Stop. No. This was Trudy we were talking about. This woman didn't like her and never had, and now she was trying to drag me into the muck with her. "I don't think that's the case. I've always had a good relationship with her."

Connie nodded, her eyes filled with what looked to be regret. "I truly hope it stays that way for you then."

"How is it with more than one baker in the family?"

"Honey, I was the original baker." She glanced away. "All of Trudy's recipes came from me."

"What?" I blurted.

She nodded. "Not her newest ones, no. Those are all

hers. But the original ones?" Connie snorted. "Those were all mine. And then I got smarter about what I shared."

If this were true...

"It's all true. Ask her and watch her face."

"That doesn't seem like her."

The woman motioned for me to follow her. "You're that lady who keeps solving cases, right?"

A sigh escaped me. "I am."

"It's hard to see the things right in front of us."

"You don't like her," I accused.

Connie didn't respond. Instead, she pointed inside the structure. "You see that?" She pointed to a large black mark on the floor. "We just poured the foundation a few days ago. Someone got wind of it and tried to set fire to the place. Fortunately, Demi was out here and saw someone running away."

"And you think Trudy did it?" I shook my head in denial. No way she did this.

"I have no proof. But someone doesn't want me to open this place. I have to have 24/7 security out here."

"That doesn't make any sense. Someone is after Trudy's business, too."

"Maybe I just got in their crosshairs. I don't really know. I haven't spoken to Trudy in close to a year now. I've poured all I have into this store and it's opening whether she likes it or not. Now, did you need anything else?"

When I shook my head, she nodded. "Alright then. I'll see you around. Best wishes on Trudy's future success."

I watched her walk away and felt decidedly uncomfortable about our conversation. She didn't sound like the kind of person who would hurt someone else.

But as I got back into my car and drove to my house, the same thought kept coming up. Trudy didn't look like the kind of person who would either.

Neither did Jen or Cole or Reese or anyone else I knew.

But someone had, and they knew where I lived and worked, so whoever this was?? They had to be a local.

FIFTEEN

The adjuster stood in front of my house staring at the front door. Hardy had sent someone over right after we'd left the first time to seal it but seeing it like this hurt my heart.

"Ms. Adair?"

"Yes. Thanks so much for coming so quickly."

He grimaced. "Sorry about the short notice on the reschedule. Something came up that I couldn't avoid."

"Not a problem. Want to head inside?"

He nodded and I unfastened the tape at the top of the door jam, moving it to the side and making a hole large enough for us to step through.

He whistled when he walked in and saw the destruction of my living room. "Someone must have been mighty angry at you."

"I'd like to find out who that was," I said with a laugh. "Maybe I could send them the bill."

The adjustor clicked his pen and walked around the

main areas of my house where all the damage had occurred. As I followed him around, I noticed more and more areas where things were broken or beyond repair. A sick feeling found and made its home in my stomach, and it got so bad, I finally had to walk outside to sit on the porch.

Hardy found me there half an hour later. He sat beside me and offered me a piece of gum. I grimaced when I saw what kind.

"Only weirdos eat cinnamon gum."

He laughed in surprise. "I don't like the kind that makes you feel like you swallowed an ice storm."

"Cinnamon gum tastes like you walked into a Hobby Lobby when they first set up all those cinnamon brooms."

Hardy snorted and popped a piece into his mouth. "I'd argue, but you're right. Those cinnamon brooms are the worst."

"They burn your nose hairs right off."

We sat in companionable silence until the adjuster came back out. He nodded to Hardy and tore a piece of paper off his clipboard. "Here's the damage amount. I'll need you to send me an itemized list of everything broken, stolen, or otherwise damaged so I can adjust this."

"How long before I can get it fixed?"

He shrugged. "Get us a few quotes. We should be able to turn it around in a day or so. Depending on the contractor's schedule, I think you could be back in your home in a month or two."

I almost swallowed my tongue. "A–what?"

Hardy put a warning hand on my knee. "Is there any way to make that a little sooner?"

He shrugged. "It isn't up to me. That's usually the amount of time it takes." His gaze turned sympathetic. "Look. You've got quite a lot of damage in there. I won't be surprised if it takes longer. You have somewhere to stay?"

"I only planned to stay a week. Two at the latest."

Hardy squeezed my knee. "She does. For as long as she needs."

"Good. I'm sorry, Ms. Adair. These things take time. If you get lucky, you can have a contractor start in the next few days." He nodded to us both and bounded down the stairs and over to his car.

Hardy and I sat in silence for a while as I digested this unfortunate turn of events.

"You can stay as long as you need to."

"I'd like to pay rent."

His gaze sharpened. "No."

"Yes."

"I don't even rent it out when it's vacant. I'm certainly not renting it out to a...friend."

"Then you'll have to let me do something." A month. That felt like eternity. I knew in the grand scheme of things it wasn't a long time, but to be away from my things and my home for that long felt like the end of the world.

"How about some of that pasta you made me before?"

I peered up at him. "Which one?"

His lips twitched. "I love pasta, so it doesn't matter to me."

"Alright then. How about tonight?"

"Sure. Want to cook in the main house or do you want me to pop over?"

The cottage felt too small for both of us because when he entered a room it felt like he sucked all the air out of it. "I'll come to you with all the groceries. You want to pick up wine?"

He rubbed the back of his neck and blushed. "I...have a wine cellar."

My eyebrows went up. "Color me green with envy. Then you pick out a nice red. Maybe I'll make alfredo."

"Sounds great." Hardy stood. "I have to get back to work. See you later?"

I nodded.

"Bye, Dakota."

Without waiting for me to respond, he walked away leaving me sitting on the porch admiring his lean back.

I DROVE BACK to the shop a few hours later to see if Poppy wanted to come home with me. Surprisingly, she hopped right into her carrier with no fuss. I called Harper right before I left, and she asked for one more day off. Since I was already slacking off pretty hard where the store was concerned, I didn't mind at all.

There were too many things on my mind and no solution to any of them. Staying at Hardy's for over a month seemed like way too much of an intrusion on his life. Yes, he'd offered. Yes, it even seemed like he meant it, but since he wouldn't accept rent, I felt like there was now an imbalance in our relationship. I didn't like to start anything out that way, so I'd have to come up with a way to pay him back. Even if it meant keeping him in fresh dinners half the year.

My phone rang just as I headed downtown. Cole was on the other end.

"Hey," he said. His voice sounded...odd.

"Everything okay?"

"I just heard something and I'm not sure how to feel about it."

"Uh oh," I said. "Is it the Silverwood Silverettes again?"

He chuckled like I hoped he would. "Nothing like that. Yet. Dakota..." his voice trailed off.

"Cole?" Concern flooded me. "Do I need to come by?"

"Not to me. But I think you should stop at the police station to see Hardy."

"Hardy? Why would I do that? I just saw him a few hours ago."

"You don't have to," Cole hedged. "But if what I heard is true, you may want to."

And on that ominous note, Cole whispered, "I'm sorry," and hung up.

The phone slipped from my fingers, and I took a quick left turn away from Hardy's house and toward the police station.

. . .

NOTHING SEEMED OUT OF PLACE. The station wasn't on fire. There were no ambulances or crime scene tape or anything that might necessitate the urgency in Cole's voice. Anger built within me as I walked inside. Did he think this was funny? Was he just being weird?

The receptionist's eyes widened when she saw me. "Oh, um, hi Dakota!"

"Hello. I'm here to see Hardy."

She looked away and down at her feet before she chewed on her lip. "He isn't available."

"You didn't even call him," I said.

"He, uh, told me he had a meeting when he came in." Color bloomed within the woman's cheeks and suspicion slowly built inside of me.

"I'll wait for him outside his office then."

I started to brush past her, but she reached out and took hold of my arm. "Ma'am! Um, Dakota. I'm sorry. I'm going to have to ask you to wait out here."

My eyes narrowed. "No thank you." I went to walk past her again and she reached for the phone. Like a snake, I pressed her hand down on the End button. "I'm not sure what's going on here, but I have a feeling I'm about to walk into something I'm not going to want to see. Warning him would make me angry. I'm asking you as a woman to hang up the phone and let me discover what this is for myself."

The woman licked her lips, her eyes darting back and forth between the hall and me. I knew I'd won when she deflated. "Okay. Fine."

"Good." I let go of her fingers and started to walk away.

"For what it's worth, I'm sure there's a good explanation."

A harsh laugh came from my throat even as acid burned within me. I didn't know what I would walk in on, but I knew from her words it wasn't going to be good.

I HEARD her voice before I saw her. Deep, husky, too intimate to be a victim or someone who wasn't already familiar with Hardy. Short saw me come in first. From the way her smile widened, I knew this would be the end. More room for her, I guess.

My steps slowed until I stood outside of his door. He didn't see me at first. His gaze was too intent on the woman.

The woman who held a dark-haired blue-eyed child.

Maybe this was his sister, my internal optimist screamed.

"She's yours," the woman said.

Maybe this was a nightmare. If I pinched myself, I would wake up.

Hardy shook his head and his gaze flicked to the adorable little girl. "If she is, there are much better ways of informing me than this."

I swallowed hard, trying my best to keep the tears from falling.

"I want to be engaged again, Hardy. We can be a family." She was stunning. Long dark hair, light brown eyes.

Slim and well dressed. Way more manicured and put together than I ever cared to be.

His eyes met mine. Grief, ragged and bright, bloomed in his eyes. Regret, followed by resignation. An entire conversation took place between us in those few seconds. Then I gathered up my courage, dried my eyes, and turned around, leaving Hardy and his potential new fiancée and child behind me.

I DIDN'T CRY until I stepped into his cottage. Poppy must have sensed something was wrong because she meowed until I picked her up, then bumped her small head against my chin. She let me hold her until I had to put her down to gather my things. My cell phone rang and rang periodically, but I ignored all the calls.

It took me twenty minutes to gather my things. A blip of time when I thought about all the effort I'd made with him. He didn't cheat on me. I didn't think he'd ever be that guy. But his sense of honor would win. I could feel it in my bones. He would choose her because there was a child involved.

And I couldn't fault him for it because giving this a chance would be in the little girl's best interest. If anything, it made me love him more.

Once I gathered my bags and left the key on the kitchen island, I stood outside the door to the cottage and drank in the fresh air. After a moment, I squared my shoulders, rolled my bag across the yard, and got in my car and drove away.

SIXTEEN

Five of the calls were from Hardy. Two of them were from Cole.

One of them was from my mother.

I called her back and didn't have to say a word. She'd already heard everything.

"There's a key under the mat, darling. Aunt Corky is over there now cleaning out the clutter from the office. I have a fold out futon in there now that's pretty comfortable, but we can see about getting you a bed if we need to."

My smile wobbled. "Thanks, Mom."

"Darling," she said and hesitated. "This too shall pass. I know it hurts and I know you must be feeling a thousand different ways, but this will pass eventually, and you'll be the stronger for it." She paused and sighed. "Until then, I'll be home in an hour with three gallons of ice cream and two bottles of wine. We'll order pizza and watch bad movies all night if you want."

"I love you," I said as I took the turn to her complex.

"I love you more, honey. I'll see you soon."

I called up Cole who didn't say much and especially didn't say I told you so and asked him to put a sign on my door keeping the shop closed tomorrow.

"I'm sorry, Dakota."

"Thank you for calling me before."

"I wasn't sure it was the right thing to do."

"It was the only thing a friend would do." I parked right in front of Mom's apartment. "Did you find anything out?"

"Not much. Connie put in for the license about four months ago. The building next to Trudy's came on the auction block two weeks ago."

"About that," I said. "We need to meet up and chat. You free tomorrow?"

The sound of flipping pages made me smile. Cole was one of the few people I knew who still used a paper calendar. "I am. How about two? Want to meet in Candlelight Springs?"

We chose a restaurant that had good soup and salad and hung up.

Closing the store tomorrow wasn't the best idea, but I'd spend the day working on getting the word out about Jeff's signing. After today, I didn't think this had anything to do with him. I still planned to pick his brain about his books, but I'd narrowed the field to a couple of people, though I still had more questions for a few people.

Tonight, though, I would hang out with my mom and cry on her shoulder.

JEN SEEMED surprised to see me. I was surprised to see myself out of bed and somewhat hydrated after the night I'd had with Mom. Fortunately, she made me drink a lot of water and stopped me after my second bowl of ice cream. I'd collapsed into bed about one a.m. and didn't wake up until nine this morning. All I had was a slight headache which I cured with a strong cup of coffee and another bottle of water Mom had shoved into my hand before I stumbled back to the office to get dressed.

As much as I tried to stop thinking about Hardy, I couldn't. The more I tried to avoid it, the more he lingered in my brain. So, I decided to try the next best thing. Avoidance.

"Morning."

"Want some coffee?" she offered.

"I'd love some."

Jen poured us both a cup. We sat down at a small table closer to the kitchen, and just as I was about to speak, Jen covered my hand with hers.

"I won't linger on this, but I heard what happened."

Tears pricked the back of my eyes.

"I'm really sorry, Dakota. That must have been difficult."

"Thank you, but I'm okay. We weren't dating or anything."

Her lips pressed together in a sad smile. "It doesn't make it hurt any less."

I exhaled a deep breath. "Regardless, I'll be okay." Forcing a smile onto my face, I asked Jen some of the questions that had been bugging me.

She answered them, though I could tell she was uncomfortable. Some were about Trudy. Some were about other things, but by the time we were finished, I had a better understanding about some things and some history I didn't know I was a part of.

As I walked out the door, I dialed Cole before heading over to see Trudy next.

MY FRIEND HELD a broom and a dustpan. Her face lit up when she saw me.

"Dakota! What a surprise." Then her expression fell when she remembered what I'm sure the entire town had been talking about since last night. "Cake?" she offered.

"No thanks. I just wanted to pop in to see how you were doing."

"Me?" she snorted. "I'm fine. The police are dragging their feet on everything and won't give me any updates. Every time I check, they tell me they'll have another update in a day or two." Trudy rolled her eyes. "But why are you here checking on me? I should be the one checking on you."

An uncharitable thought rose in me. She should have, shouldn't she? Had it always been like this? Had the woman blinded me with delicious baked goods rather than genuine friendship?

Maybe she had, but that didn't mean she had anything to do with the murder in her shop. And I had so many personal things pop up that I hadn't even bothered to look more into the girl and who she was or who she'd been before she'd met such an untimely end.

I felt like a failure, through and through. Had I failed myself most of all?

I'd never been great at making friends even though I really wanted them. The introvert curse, I guess.

"It's not a big deal," I said casually. "The shop is closed today, but I still have a few things to do to get ready for the signing."

"Signing?" Trudy kept sweeping.

I watched her. "Jeff Martins is coming."

The broom slipped from her hands. "Oh! Wow! What a boon." She frowned and let out a harsh breath of air. "I'm so clumsy, I swear!"

"I didn't think I could get him, but he agreed. Once he's here, I think I'm going to grill him about that scene in the book."

Trudy winced and turned her back to me. "Do you think that's such a good idea? I don't think he'd like getting questioned about a murder he had nothing to do with."

I shrugged. "I dunno. I wonder if he might be the kind of guy who'd love to get his hands into another mystery. After all, a copycat might be just the thing he needs to get some more ideas flowing."

Trudy kept sweeping. "I think the police have this in hand, Dakota. I don't think you'll be able to help any more than you've already done."

I tilted my head and watched her nervous swipes with the broom. "Really? I've found out quite a bit since I started doing some digging."

She paused a hair too long before she kept sweeping. "Oh?"

"Why didn't you tell me Connie was opening her own shop?"

Trudy's knuckles went white on the broom. She forced a laugh. "I didn't think she'd last more than a month or two. It didn't seem important."

"I think it would be. If you think someone might be after your business, I would have looked after everyone."

"If it's her, she won't last long," she snapped. "No one will last long up against my offerings."

The words were so...arrogant and so out of place coming from her. Maybe I'd never known her at all.

"Maybe so," I said as I rose from the chair. "Anyway, I just wanted to let you know I turned over everything I had to the police."

She stilled and slowly turned around. "You did?"

"Of course I did. Who else would I have told?"

Trudy's eyes flashed. "Me maybe?"

I laughed and slowly edged my way to the door. Her eyes followed me. For the first time, I felt a frisson of unease slide down my spine. "I don't have too much. This is one case the police are going to have to finish up."

Her shoulders relaxed. "Well then, thanks for trying, Dakota. The offer of cake is still open."

I patted my stomach. "Not today, I think. Mom fed me a gallon of ice cream last night."

I shoved open the door with my hip and hurried out. With my other hand, I dug my cell phone out and called Cole.

"Can you record this?" I asked him.

"Go," Cole said.

I told him everything I knew.

SEVENTEEN

The sound of sirens lit up the silent morning about ten minutes later. I quietly gathered my things, flipped the lights off, and slipped outside, taking the back way on the drive back to Mom's.

Once I was on the open road, I dialed the number for the surveillance company who handled my cameras and asked them to upgrade my plan to 24/7 surveillance. They readily agreed and I breathed a sigh of relief. I'd had them installed a while ago, but I only kept them on from 6:30 p.m. to 6:30 a.m. The cost would double now, but it was worth it.

I sent Reese a quick note to thank him again and warn him about what was coming. Trudy was bidding against herself. She'd set up the VPN and a new account to try to make it look like someone was trying to open up a competing business right next door. I didn't understand everything she'd done. Some of it seemed too far-fetched to believe, but after speaking to Reese and to Connie, I had to wonder if poor Tara had found out about what Trudy was doing and paid the price.

I still couldn't see my friend committing a crime like that. Jealousy and pride drove people to do some pretty crazy things, but murder?

I couldn't see it, but no one else had presented themselves on a platter to me, and honestly, I was so mentally and emotionally exhausted right now, I had to turn the rest over to the police.

Tonight, I planned to get a good night's sleep.

I'd be at the bank first thing tomorrow morning to pay off the shop.

MY PHONE RANG AT MIDNIGHT. Bleary eyed, I rolled over and answered.

"Hullo?"

"We need you down at Tattered Pages," Hardy said.

I blinked and was suddenly wide awake. "M'kay," I said and clicked off.

I made it there in record time.

Two police cruisers sat in front of the store with their lights flashing. I scrambled out of my car, pulling my cardigan closer over my pajama tank, and rushed over to where Hardy stood. A man lay on the ground, cuffed and watched by Short.

Her lips thinned as she glanced at me, but I thought I saw a flash of pity there.

"We caught him with a gallon of gasoline and a box of matches," Hardy said.

My hand fluttered to my throat. "How? I have surveillance set up and I didn't get a call."

Hardy looked away. Short's gaze lingered on him before she addressed me. "*Someone* suggested we put surveillance on your shop. We caught him walking up the main street." She put a foot on his back. "Idiot," she muttered.

"You were planning on burning down my shop?!" I shrieked down at the man. I still couldn't see his face, but when she rolled him over, I stopped in my tracks.

"You're Trudy's nephew!"

A voice came from behind me, making me jerk. "And my daughter's fiancé."

"Jen?"

She stared down at the man with a grim look. "I never liked him. He started dating my daughter several months ago." Jen glanced over at Trudy's shop. "I knew what Trudy was planning to do for a while now, though I never thought she'd go this far."

"She was going to make me a partner!" the nephew spat.

Hardy glanced over at me. "We took Trudy into custody early last night."

"I figured," I said.

He fidgeted and touched my arm. "Can we talk for a second?"

Short's face hardened, but she looked away.

"For a moment," I said and followed him over to the bench in front of my store.

He sat down and I followed but scooted down to the opposite side. A broken laugh escaped him. "I've made a right mess of things, haven't I?"

"It isn't your fault." It wasn't. Not exactly. He couldn't help the timing, nor were his prior relationships his fault nor any of my business.

"I sent out DNA." His jaw tightened and he looked away. "All I ever wanted was someone like you."

I didn't say a word.

"She was a mistake. A youthful dalliance that turned into something more. All I wanted was a family, and I thought she could give it to me..."

"You don't have to justify anything to me."

He scrubbed a hand through his hair. "I know, but I want you to understand."

A sad smile flickered over my lips. "That's the problem, Hardy. I do understand."

Hope flared in his eyes, doused by my head shake. "I need more. I want more." I tilted my face up to the sky. "But I don't think you can give it to me."

He said nothing else. Instead, he curled his fingers over mine and we sat that way until Short had gathered Trudy's nephew and stuffed him into the car and drove away. I stood a few minutes after that and dug my keys out.

"You didn't have to leave, you know," Hardy said.

"I did and you know it."

He swallowed and looked up. "I know," he whispered.

I bent down and brushed a kiss over his forehead. "I'll see you around, Hardy."

He cupped his hand around the back of my neck and held me there for a moment before he released me. "I love you, Dakota."

My willpower almost broke. I was a dam standing there, trying to hold strong against a hurricane battering at my defenses. I pulled away and stood up, memorizing the lines and planes of his face before I turned around and hurried to my car.

EIGHTEEN

It wasn't much of a relief to know Trudy wasn't a murderer when I found out she'd put her nephew up to it. Three long weeks had passed. I'd paid off Tattered Pages and given Harper another raise. I told her this time if she wanted another one, she might have to find another job. I'd only been partially kidding.

A For Sale sign had gone up in front of *Sprinkle Heaven* two days ago. I hadn't yet paid off my mortgage, so I still had money in the bank. The auction was canceled, and the property had gone back up on the market. I eyed the listing every single day and not one person had bid on it.

24 hours blipped on the timer. If I put a bid in, there was a good chance I could expand Tattered Pages. Or...I could open a new business.

"You're cheating again," I said to Daniel.

An enigmatic grin appeared on his face. "But you still

don't know how I'm doing it, so once again, am I really cheating?"

We sat in front of the chess board, a half-eaten pizza to the right of us. We'd polished off half a bottle of wine, and I still couldn't beat him at chess.

Daniel and I were still friends, thankfully. He hadn't pushed me for anything at all. There was no doubt in my mind he'd heard about what happened. One thing I really liked about him was he never pushed boundaries out of respect and possibly some strong boundaries of his own. I'd tell him what happened in my own time.

Until then, I was content to let him keep cheating at chess.

I hadn't heard from Hardy since that night in front of my shop. My house was still in the throes of repair, so my mom was still housing me. Daniel offered to let me stay, but that was a complication I wasn't ready for and wasn't sure I ever would be.

One thing this entire episode taught me? I liked the simplicity of being single. Emotions took it out of me. I liked books. Chess. Eating whatever I wanted. Coming home whenever I wanted.

And my cat.

Poppy was grumpy but there for me. And though she didn't have much to do with solving this case, she still hung out with me when she sensed I was about to do something foolish again.

Like cry over Hardy.

Those days were slowly lessening and for that I was

thankful. I was better than crying over a man, wasn't I? The town was all abuzz with the new woman in Hardy's life. He'd stayed mum over the results of the DNA, though since she was still around, I had to believe the results had shown him his youthful indiscretion had become a permanent fixture in his life.

I had to hand it to him. The little girl was beautiful and sweet. I'd heard stories of her around town, though I stayed away from anywhere he might be.

Daniel grinned at me and made his next move. "I was thinking."

"Oh?" I said and grimaced as I saw his Queen sitting right in front of my King.

"You should name your new PI firm Turning Pages."

My gaze flew up just as Daniel knocked my King over. "Checkmate."

A Shelf Indulgence Cozy Mystery Series

How about a ghost whisperer in a new magical town? Check out
The Psychic Cleaner series!

Psychic Cleaner

Like a little more magic with your cozies? Check out The
Magical Soapmaker Mysteries!

The Magical Soapmaker Mysteries

If you'd like a little more action and sass and don't mind some
PG-13 language, check out my Aphrodite series.

The Goddess Chronicles

Or, if you like a snarky bartender with a secretive mixed heritage,
meet Violet!

Cocktails in Hell

ABOUT THE AUTHOR

Sheryl likes cake too much and can be found hoarding it while hiding from her children in the pantry closet.

Follow her on Amazon at: https://www.amazon.com/S-E-Babin/e/B00J1J236A